avalon 11/73

w

13.00

THE TRAIL
OF
MYTHMAKER

THE TRAIL
OF
MYTHMAKER

•

TRACY DUNHAM

AVALON BOOKS
THOMAS BOUREGY AND COMPANY, INC.
401 LAFAYETTE STREET
NEW YORK, NEW YORK 10003

PRINTED IN THE UNITED STATES OF AMERICA
ON ACID-FREE PAPER
BY HADDON CRAFTSMEN, SCRANTON, PENNSYLVANIA

For Skyler and Jessie Gemmer,
who will create their own myths.

Prologue

On October 7, 1868, a peace commission met in Chicago, Illinois. The question presented to assembled important persons was simple: What do we do with the Indians? The Medicine Lodge Treaty, it was clear, had either been misunderstood or ignored by many of the tribes signing it. Some commentators have suggested that the terms were improperly translated to the chiefs who signed the document. Others have explained that the chiefs, while understanding the words, did not have a clear comprehension of their import—in other words, they did not understand that they had given up their rights to all but a bit of their traditional hunting grounds, and that they would be permitted to hunt outside the boundaries of their respective reservations only with governmental approval.

For the Plains Indians, such restrictions were not only futile, they were ridiculous. As the Kiowa chief Satanta said at the time of the signing of the treaty, "We don't want to settle—I love to roam over the

1

prairie; there I am free and happy.'' They didn't stop roaming, not some of them. The Kiowa and Comanche rode like locusts through Texas, south of the Arkansas River, while the Cheyenne fought through Kansas. The generals, all seasoned Civil War veterans, knew of only one solution.

Generals William Tecumseh Sherman, Harney, Augur, and Terry held sway at the Chicago Peace Commission. With a temperament that had waged war on the civilian population of Georgia, Sherman convinced the commission to order that all tribes which had signed the Medicine Lodge Treaty must stay within their reservation boundaries. There was to be no hunting outside those imaginary lines. Tribesmen caught off the reservation were to be punished—swiftly and with hot lead.

The next ten years were to be a time when the tribes either starved on the reservations, or defied the Army and returned to their way of life on the prairie, eating their horses when the buffalo were gone. Many Kiowa chiefs were sent to die at Fort Marion Prison in Florida. Satanta committed suicide in a Texas penitentiary. Many more died fighting the U.S. Army. But in the end, Sherman's way carried the day, and life was hell for the Plains Indians caught between the mortar of a moving white population and the pestle of the yellow-legged horse soldiers.

Chapter 1

Why do white men always build with sharp angles? Square houses, square beds, square tables, rectangular fireplaces. Nothing in harmony in a white man's house, no circles of peace with the world as it is. I long for my tepee. The white man's world is all hard edges, all pain. I have chosen to come back to it, to wear its pain.

I am Elizabeth McFarland, wife of Johnny Two Hats, sister of Noble McFarland, daughter of Colonel John McFarland. I have carried the square wooden table Noble made for me from old ammunition boxes outside, where I can feel the sun on my face and free myself, for these moments at least, from the fetters of the square house Noble built for me. No, I am not complaining, he has been more than kindness to me. The house is tiny and snug, and nestles low on a hill where I can stand and search the horizon every day for signs of my husband. Noble doesn't like for me to call Johnny my husband, so I have learned to leave his name out of our brief conversations.

Noble brought me ink and paper, a heavy foolscap that must have cost him a fortune out here, from the sutler's at Fort Larned. He didn't ask why I wanted it, and I didn't say. I position my square stool and my square table so I can face the southwest and feel the sun soaking into my black dress, buttoned so tightly over my corset. The corset is my punishment, my hair shirt if you will, my reminder that I must pretend to be white for my brother's sake.

I have noticed the immigrants, the white soldiers at the fort who were not stationed there when my father was, staring at my left hand with its missing finger. My face will never lose its sun-wrinkles, my body its hard leanness. All those years of starvation took their toll, and these voluminous skirts, these petticoats and bloomers, these high necks and long sleeves, can never hide my past with the Kiowa. I do not want them to. But for Noble's sake, I try.

Noble and Rebecca asked me to live with them, but I could not. Their five children, red-haired and exuberant, would have killed me simply by their presence. I would have destroyed their peace and harmony, and I managed somehow to convey enough of the truth to Noble that he built me this house. He ordered lumber, not content with sod for his sister. The wood has weathered to a soft gray, and sometimes I feel I could blend into its walls so easily and become a part of its swirls and knots if only I could shut my eyes. But I cannot do that, I must keep watch.

The wind is picking up, as it does every afternoon

in early autumn, and from habit, I cup my good right hand over my eyes and squint to see as far as I can. I know it is hopeless, but I do so more from habit now, more than anything else. The breeze flattens my black skirts to my legs, flapping them uselessly like fighting crows. I splay my maimed left hand to my chest, to feel my heart still beating. I have never been able to give up, not even when death seemed my only friend.

But I must get to work. One day someone will read these writings, and know there was a white woman who loved the Kiowa as her own people, a woman who chose to live a life that was dying even as she found it. This woman loved a half-breed Comanche she'd known since childhood, and freely followed his path in life. This woman, an outcast among her own kind, cannot give up hope.

I have dipped the steel-tipped pen in the well and written my name at the top of the pale paper. I hesitate, wondering for a second if I should line out what I have already written. But the first words are the truth. My name is Mythmaker. I am a member of Kicking Bird's clan, of the Kiowa.

Chapter 2

I remember that winter so well. Johnny and I crept away from Medicine Lodge Creek, leaving the hundreds of tepees of my people in the middle of the night. I wanted no harsh words with my father, the colonel. Most of all, I desired no repercussions against my people. We are called Kiowa by the white man, a name meaning "enemy." We call ourselves members of Kicking Bird's clan, for I have become one of them after my capture. Noble was younger then, and couldn't even begin to understand why I chose to stay with the People, my people. I'm not sure he fully comprehends my decision even now, but at least he's no longer furious with me. We've come far, in these hard years between October of 1867 and today.

Johnny Two Hats and I slipped from the encampment like badgers through their underwater doorways, seeking nocturnal protection. Riding hard, we didn't sleep until the next time a sliver of moon slipped from behind the clouds, and then only a few hours.

Wrapped in Johnny's blanket, we fit together like spoons, the horses' reins wrapped around Johnny's wrist. I know he slept with part of himself watching over us, while I snored like a buffalo. It was very embarrassing for our first time together.

He knew where he was taking me. Actually, it was to hide me, for he knew full well that white women captives were valuable to their Indian captors, even though the whites might despise them once returned. They could still be ransomed for extra baubles, flour, or maybe even a rifle left over from the War. Johnny Two Hats also knew that the soldiers didn't care a dead dog for a half-breed former scout. I hated it, running from my father, my brother, my old life, but we both knew it had to be done.

In the year during which he and Noble had sought me, he'd returned to his mother's people, the Comanche, and found himself in the bargain. No longer was he a half-breed scout for hire, but his mother's son with proud Comanche blood, and my protector, should my father, the colonel, disbelieve Noble's story of my death. Unless my father was taken in by my brother's lies, he would be honor bound to send out more search parties.

The small band where Johnny made his home never came to the Medicine Lodge Treaty councils. Perhaps Johnny had warned them that white men never kept their word and would try to steal their land, but he never told me. As I waited for Johnny on a low ridge line somewhere south of Kansas, not knowing exactly where I was except under God's blue sky, I could see the scalp locks floating in the breeze from lodge poles.

I know only too well I could have been nothing more than bones on the prairie and hair on a pole, but Johnny had taught me much in our childhood together on the Army post. What he taught me, gave me the strength and the wits to survive my capture. Nothing I'd learned in boarding school back East had done that. Pulling my blanket closer to my shoulders, I shivered at the memories of the hard winter I almost froze to death, a nonperson within the tribe, a crazy woman who'd been spared her life but was left with nothing to live for.

I sensed instantly that these people of Johnny's were a warrior people. That afternoon in late fall when you know winter will harden your belly soon, the sky was as blue as the necklaces I have seen made by the Navajo. Prairie grass, flattened by the tribe in its daily path to and from the river, was almost as golden as my hair as a child. I had left my people, my foster son, my foster father, to be with the man I love. I was a white woman in a Comanche war camp. I should have been afraid, but I was far beyond fear.

I was glad my foster son, Magpie, and his grandfather had returned to the Kiowa when we left. I did not yet want a son who would make war. I thought I could teach peace, and how to get along with the whites, even how to succeed in their world. Oh, I was such an infant in my knowledge!

Using sign language, which I understood a little, Johnny told his people my name, Mythmaker. Fortunately, they had heard stories and I soon found myself surrounded by chattering women, bemoaning, I gathered dimly, Johnny's lack of preparation for a new wife. I had never before thought of myself as his wife, not until they threw their hands in despair as they led me to his tepee, promising help so that I would not be a disgrace to my man or his people. I did not like to make light of their concern, or explain that my house-keeping skills in a tepee were minimal. Soon enough, they would come to know my value lay in my healing work.

I don't know how much more I should write of my early days with the Comanche, and with my husband. I do not want these words to hurt Noble, or his family, should they read them someday after I am gone. Perhaps I will burn this foolscap in a roaring bonfire, a conflagration worthy of a victory dance in the village of my people. The moment the last word is written, I will jerk my corset off and toss it in the fire with my writing. Then I will follow them both. I must think on this. What do I have to live for, a woman of the People with no people left to love?

But first, I must tell my story, at least to myself.

Chapter 3

Indian agent Jesse Leavenworth hated February in the Indian Territory. The godforsaken wind cut through his Chicago-cut coat as if it was made of paper, and he swore his toes would never thaw. It was 1868—another year he was responsible for the red man, for making them behave like civilized folks. This time the government had seen fit to give him the Kiowa-Comanche Reservation, the land the Medicine Lodge Treaty said *belonged*—and he snickered at the word—to the tribes. His home and his work were in the Eureka Valley, not much of a stone's throw from old Fort Cobb. Thank goodness, he thought, the Wichita at least, whose reservation was nearby, were a peaceful people. Maybe they'd be a good influence on these terrifyingly warlike savages who were now in his charge.

He settled into his office, hung pictures of General Grant and George Washington, and watched the winter sky from his glass-paned window. The Medicine

10

Lodge Treaty called for no food allotments, so he didn't expect to hear from his charges anytime soon. Spring would be soon enough to introduce himself to the Kiowa and Comanche. Shuffling papers on his desk, cursing the ink blot which had stained his cuff, he almost broke out in hives at the sight from his window that February afternoon.

My Lord have mercy, he prayed as he pulled himself together.

"Mr. Leavenworth, Mr. Leavenworth!" His gasping secretary flung himself into his inner sanctum. "I think you'd better come quickly, sir!"

Agent Leavenworth drew himself upright, straightened his collar points, gave his tie a quick smooth, and shrugged into his jacket. Heaven only knew how so many of them got so close to his building, without an alarm going up. How did so many Indians appear on his doorstep so quietly? Another quick glance out the window, an assessment of the panic in his secretary's face, and Agent Leavenworth reminded himself he represented the United States government on this land, and was a powerful man.

The silent line of Kiowa and Comanche formed a winding circle around the agent's buildings, their women a mute backdrop to the more colorfully garbed men astride wiry little horses. Agent Leavenworth stopped on the front stoop of his building, grasping the porch support forcefully in one hand, keeping the other tucked in his trousers pocket. He would not let them see him flinch. Despite his apprehension, he had to admit they were a handsome people. *There must be hundreds,* he thought, *and they want something from me.* Indians always wanted something from the white man. When will they learn? he wondered.

"Get my interpreter, man," he hissed at his secretary.

Smiling, Leavenworth raised his one arm quickly in the universal gesture of greeting, as if to say, See, I have no weapon in my hand, I will not harm you. An old man, a chief, Leavenworth surmised, prodded his pony in the ribs and rode forward. Studying the man's carefully beaded leggings, the soft, supple skins that made up his old-fashioned outfit, Leavenworth knew he was dealing with a man of some importance, perhaps a medicine man. There was no touch of the white man here, no calico shirt, no cowman's hat.

Leavenworth was bowled over as the old man began speaking in English.

"We have come for food. The food promised us by the treaty." The old man's voice was strong, and Leavenworth could hear him from where he stood, rooted to the front stoop.

Puzzled, Leavenworth searched quickly in his memory for anything he could have overlooked in his duties to these savages. He was a careful man, and he knew he had not overlooked a matter as important as food.

"There is none. The treaty did not say you would get food here. You are permitted to hunt buffalo on this land, on your reservation."

The old man, his thick white hair lifted by a winter gust of wind, turned his head to speak to the hundred who spread out to his sides. Leavenworth cringed at the guttural inflections of their language, hating its sound. He felt much the same about German, which he considered an ugly language. His reverie was pierced by a low, hateful-sounding response, riding the crest of the horsemen like a tornado.

He knew fury when he heard it. The old man lifted his hand for silence, and got it. Leavenworth was impressed.

"My people were told to come to the agent for food this winter. This is no mistake." The old man spoke as if the white man's words he proclaimed were truth itself, and he was incapable of error.

"There is no food." Leavenworth didn't know how he could be plainer speaking. Clearly, these people didn't believe him. What was he to do? Grasping for any solution, he smiled. "But I will wire the Army, and see what they say."

Sending a telegram would not only alert the troops to the demand, he would make sure he had protection. He didn't trust any of these Kiowa or Comanche; there was no telling how they'd react to his denial of responsibility for feeding them. Pins and needles pricked his feet, and he shivered in the winter wind. The dark faces staring down at him looked cut from oak, their expressions so fierce in repose that fear coursed down his spine.

Despite his trepidation, he twirled and marched back into his office. Finding his secretary not far behind, he snapped about, barking, "Where is that blasted interpreter, anyway?"

The man shrugged, wild-eyed as he slammed the door behind them both. "No telling, those half-breeds have no sense of duty, sir."

Leavenworth sighed. "I pity those of us who do." He wondered if the security of a government job was going to be enough to hold him to this desolate land and these wild people. If they didn't like his answer when it came from the Army, and he knew they wouldn't, there was no telling what would happen. Actually, he felt in his bones he knew he couldn't control them. He knew what would happen. He hadn't seen evidence himself, but he'd heard.

Shutting off the horror pictures in his mind, Agent Leavenworth sat down to draft his telegram to General Sherman. With this bunch, he wasn't going to fool around, he was going to the top to make sure he had his derriere protected.

Chapter 4

These are troubled times, she mused as she flipped
the dripping sheet over the line strung from the nail
pounded in her wooden door frame to the pole Harry'd
dug into the ground a few feet away. Troubled times
for Texas. She liked the alliteration. Didn't know what
got her going today, maybe it was doing laundry with
a feel of wet to the air and dark clouds tumbling over
themselves on the horizon. A tinge of cold added to
her discomfort, and she cursed herself for a fool for
doing laundry today. But it was Monday, and she
couldn't break her work pattern just because of some
bad weather coming.

More than the sky ate at her peace of mind. Harry'd
left her the shotgun, loaded and propped by the
clothesline, when he rode off early to check the stock.
He had a way about him, an aching in the bones, that
warned him when trouble was coming. Herself, she
wasn't so inclined to look for worry, it would find her
soon enough. Like if she didn't get these sheets up to

dry in the stiff wind that cut havoc with her ability to get the pins on the fabric.

But Harry had made his point, jamming shells in the shotgun with his thumb. Better to be ready, should it happen. They lived with the knowledge that the tribes were not abiding by the treaty terms from just a few months before, and it was, as Harry said, a matter of time. Cheyenne were lifting scalps in Kansas, and the Kiowa wouldn't let them have all the fun, Harry said. She didn't let herself think about what "it" was. Stories told by other settlers scared her witless, when they first stopped their Conestoga and staked their land. Now, after a couple of years, she felt her fear like a bad hangnail—annoying but nothing to get upset about.

Until today. Harry's grim look, the pains he took to clean the rifle, the handgun, and the shotgun had her good and worried. She paused in her work, her face to the wind, her hands rough and red with the lye soap. She'd be lucky to get the laundry dry, it would have to be strung in the dugout, with the sod roof to shower dirt all over her efforts at keeping them clean and civilized. If she'd been another type of woman, she'd have used a word she'd heard the cowboys in town use when they were drunk and reeling in the streets.

The rise before her fluttered. Quail, maybe, she thought. Just a flutter of feathers, a hop here and there. But something made her edge over to the shotgun, her eyes stuck on the rise as if it was about to produce gold. Flapping in another sudden cold, wet gust, the sheets enveloped her for a second. Fighting her way free, she found herself panting hard. Now the hill was unnaturally still. She expected some more movement, if it had been quail. Where was Harry? Would he hear her fire the shotgun in time? The hill remained still, too still after the commotion she'd seen just seconds before. If a prairie dog was after a bird, there'd be squawking galore, angry chatter. She thought of Harry's premonition, decided she'd pay attention to him, for today, anyhow. Her stomach tightened, and with hands like ice, she tried to inch nonchalantly toward the house. Her feet wouldn't move.

She gave up any semblance of composure and dived for the shotgun, skidding in the dust beside the dugout. Wiping her eyes clear with the corner of her apron, she clutched the weapon to her chest with the other hand. A nervous twitter arose in the field not far from where she'd first seen the flutter of movement. Blast her sheets, and blast her husband for leaving her alone. Scrambling through the door to the dugout, she swung the wood shut behind her, grabbing for the stout oak bar Harry'd made form a plank in their wagon. After she slammed it through the iron braces Harry'd forged, she flew to the one window, whose oil paper covering was next to useless. Scrounging under the tablecloth, she hauled out the wooden cover and threw it into place. Locking it with the pins made of nails, she rocked back on her heels and took a deep breath. She comforted herself with the thought that Harry'd sense what was happening, he'd come soon.

Sliding back the catch that held the cover on the rifle hole, she peered into her yard. It was the same gray sky, same lowering clouds, same clothesline with her sheets now hanging limply. Just as she began to relax and chide herself for such foolishness, the wind rose again, this time telling her she'd been right. The scent it carried was earthy, rich like the animal fat she used to make soap. It didn't come from anything growing in the ground around their dugout, that much she was sure of.

Forcing the hammer back on the shotgun, she poked the barrel through the hole, just an inch or so, enough so she could swivel and shoot when she had to. She remembered Harry's lessons, how she should exhale just before she shot so she wouldn't jiggle too much aiming at the target. Squeeze slowly, make each barrel count, she reminded herself. Resting her finger on the trigger, she tried to see around the barrel into the yard. She couldn't make out much, just her sheets. Blast them, she thought, they could be used to hide someone creeping up on her. Why had she insisted on doing the wash today, of all days? The double-barreled shotgun was an old but trusty friend, and she knew she could pull the trigger to kill an Indian. She hoped to make both barrels count, before she had to reload.

Shells! The rest of the shells were on top of the mantel, and she'd forgotten to get them. Reluctant to give up her post now that she'd established herself, she glanced quickly behind her. The tongue of the wagon had made a sturdy mantel, and she wished it barred her door along with the oak she'd locked into place. But the darned thing wouldn't walk over to her and hand her the shells, and she reckoned she'd better get them before she was desperate.

Sliding the shotgun on its butt, she lunged for the mantel. Just as she turned to shake the shells into her apron pocket, the door came flying at her as though it had been kicked by a mule. For a second, she stood speechless, staring at the hole where it had been, the tattered leather hinges flapping like a dog hungry for slops. Harry's carefully done metalcraft swung from one nail like a metronome. For a second, she remembered playing the piano, back East, and wondered if she'd ever do so again.

Nothing happened for what seemed to her like hours. Slowly she shifted her eyes from the useless door to the shotgun, knocked sideways by the force of whatever blew the door literally off its hinges. Realizing she'd held her breath since the crash, she slowly exhaled, and tried to reach for the weapon. But something held her back, and she was useless to fight against it. Suddenly, she knew what kept her away from anywhere near the door, as a blur of a man, half-naked, face painted wildly in red and black, swung through in a motion so fluid she was reminded of water running.

She wondered who was screaming, then realized it was herself, as she dived for the bed and any protection it could offer. Again, she smelled the animal fat, only this time mixed with fear, then her own urine as the Indian seized her by her neck with a grip that shook the breath out of her. She would never play the piano again, she thought, as all she saw before her eyes were her sheets, trampled in the dirt under the feet of painted horses ridden by naked men. Why had she done laundry today? she wondered.

Chapter 5

I hate this place, I realized now, staring at the worn paths between the tepees. Everything is brown and black and tan, and I crave the color of laughter, the silver shining in Grandfather's hair.

I have dropped my basket, my desperate attempt to blend in. I am more alone now, among the Comanche, than when Johnny first smuggled me from the Kiowa camp on the Medicine Lodge grounds and the two of us left Grandfather and Magpie to go on alone.

Let them see me weep. I defy the bustling women who carry baskets of berries on their hips and their heads. I pressed my palms to my cheeks, reluctant to shame Johnny. I cannot make Comanche talk well yet, and my frustration bubbles within me like bad broth.

A few chokeberries cling to branches, this late in the season. I wondered at the lateness of the pemmi-can-making, but didn't ask. I can only guess why the women hadn't had much time to put up the layers of buffalo fat and dried berries. The men had been raiding, and they'd been on the move, often and fast. Now, with winter well and truly on its way, the Comanche felt safe enough from the bluecoats to put down for a while. The tepees have the feel of permanency now, as though settling into the brown earth before the snows fly.

Then the offal pile grew, the winter grasses matted under constant traffic, and I feel no longer content just to be with Johnny. I need more to my life than the endless drudgery of a woman. I bend to dust off the berries before settling them back in the basket. No one has noticed my unseemly show of emotion, or else they are too polite to mention it. I am still a stranger here, although Johnny's friends and their women try to make me feel at home. But what is home to someone like me, who has turned her back on the civilized structures of the white man? I remember my tepee with Grandfather and Magpie, the lessons in reading and writing I devised for the boy to make the long winter days go more quickly. Among the Kiowa, I was not just another woman, I was Mythmaker, seer and healer, prophet and sage. My position protected me from this endless toil I find myself burdened with to keep my husband and his home clean and food on the fire. I find myself daydreaming of teaching my young Kiowa charges, educating them for the day when the white men run through their camps like locusts, devouring their way of life.

These Comanche are much like my Kiowa, at least from what Johnny tells me. Racing their spare little horses, shaggy-furred and surefooted, they raid the Plains like Genghis Khan. I know this and, in a way, admire them, their stern code and harsher honor. I cannot feel through their iron wall of self-discipline, to sense the people within, not yet. Perhaps this is because I do not yet speak their language well enough. It was not like that with the Kiowa; I could see their hearts quickly, once I surrendered my white sense of self and became one with them.

Today is my day for sorrow, I can see that now. Johnny rode out to hunt, and I am bereft without his company. He has been all I have wanted in a husband, and I find I search still for his face in the camp as he throws the bones with the men or whittles on his pipe. One smile from him and I feel at peace again. But today he has promised to stay gone until he brings home meat. We are beginning to hunt this area bare, we have camped so long. The Comanche are a voracious people, eating like wolves when there is food. I wonder how they bear the lean winter months? I suppose I shall find out.

My reverie is snapped by a cry from the distance. High trills join it from the camp, and I begin to understand what is happening. The men who rode out before we came to the camp must have returned, for suddenly women and children pour into the prairie like ants racing for spilled honey. Carefully, I secure my basket of berries inside our tepee and slip into the crowd racing for the men I can now see in the distance. The legs of their ponies dance, and I can see flutters like ribbons snapping on poles held aloft in the afternoon breeze. I am surprised how many horses there seem to be, then realize that this is a raiding party, and they have been successful. Horses are a sign of wealth among the Comanche, as with the Kiowa. Many tepees will be much wealthier tonight, I surmise. But how can I warn Johnny's people, as I have my own, that ponies and stolen blankets will not give them the tools they need to survive the onslaught of the whites? They will never believe my bleak words. I am not one of them, and I am not sure I ever can be. Johnny will have to be the one to explain, I decide as I turn to go back to my home, suddenly eager to leave the gay scene I know will ensue once the men are back in camp.

But I am not fast enough. The women by the stream have heard the cry, and running as quickly as they can in their straight-skirted gowns, they grab my arms and pull me like some helpless child with them. I tumble along in the gravity of their joy, loath to jerk free and so set myself apart. I wish I had.

The vision before me is clear still. Painted for war, the men are a maze of red and black paint, their ponies painted with symbols of valor and coup. I was just beginning to surrender to amazement at such a colorful scene, when one particularly colorful steed pranced before me. A piebald, his white and brown splotches were splayed with red hands. Grinning, I waved to this fanciful vision's rider, when my eyes traveled involuntarily upward. At the point of the long, warlike lance flew the trophies captured by this particular warrior. Accustomed as I was to scalps among the Kiowa, I should have been inured to such a gruesome sight. Yet not once among Kicking Bird's clan had I ever seen such a long trail of blond, some woman's pride and joy, probably lovingly brushed a thousand strokes each night. Perhaps the owner's husband had helped her with such glorious hair, taking the brush from her hands and adding his strokes to her shining tresses. I shuddered to think what had happened to the white woman who once possessed this stunning trophy. Pressing the heels of my palms to my eyes, I fought back the tears. I hadn't wept once since sneaking away from Kicking Bird's camp. I had no idea why that long furl of blond should be my undoing, but I could no longer stand to be among the Comanche.

Running for our tepee, I had no plan to pack. Jerking out our parfleche, I stuffed whatever was at hand inside. My hands trembled as I gathered my few belongings: my painted comb, my quill made from a goose feather, hollowed for me by Johnny just recently so I could write with berry ink on bits of old leather. The moccasins I have been softening for Johnny, and the copper pot, a gift to us from Johnny's friends, I will leave. I am in such a state I can think only hurry, hurry, run, flee, do not stay here a second longer!

I'm too late. A woman, older and with a kindly face I recognize, scratches politely at our tepee door and lifts the corner. When I hesitate, she ducks her head, and I see tears coursing her leathered cheeks. I know enough to ask if I can be of assistance.

"My man," she answers simply, "has been hurt." At least, that's what I thought she said. Frowning, I wonder what she wants from me. Then I realize that Johnny must have told some of his friends of my healing gifts. Do I want to help these people? I wonder briefly. Then I know I must: they are Johnny's mother's tribe, I owe them. They have given him what he needed, when he needed to find me. I realize her husband must have been one of the men returning in triumph. Gesturing at my body, I ask her, "Where?" Jabbing at her thigh, she gestures for me to hurry. But first she points, and pulls her finger back as though it were on a trigger, then again, at her thigh. I understand.

Grabbing my small bag of herbs, I scramble out the door to race behind her. She is flying, and I comprehend her urgency. A bullet wound that has festered has all the makings of tragedy, especially if gangrene has set in. I'd seen it in the Army hospitals when I was a girl on post. I felt in my belt for the small woman's knife I carried with me always, and wondered if it would do the job. If only Johnny were back, I mumbled to myself, he could translate for me. But I was on my own this time.

I could tell this one was going to be trouble. A fierce-looking warrior, he was barely conscious but still snarling incoherently. The wound raged red even from a distance. He must have been in excruciating pain, but all I could sense from him was anger. How could I explain that such fury would not help him heal?

Lunging as I approached, he snarled what I knew must be epithets at me. His wife ran to his side and tried to soothe his brow, as though his words were only the rantings of an invalid. I knew better. This man hated white-eyes, and that was all he saw when he saw me. His wife mumbled to him rapidly, but I caught Johnny's Comanche name. She must have thought explaining my presence in their tribe would calm him, but he uttered one final word, whose interpretation could not be misunderstood by even the most innocent.

Staring down at him, I had to decide whether or not to take the case. If I failed, would his death in any way diminish my husband's stature among his tribesmen? Would I too be condemned? I had wondered at the absence of a medicine man in camp, and staring at the man before me, I knew why there'd been none. This man, seething with unspeakable hatred for me, was the medicine man.

I did what I have always done in moments like this—I prayed. Rocking back on my heels, I shut my eyes and denied the picture of hatred before me. After all, I reasoned, the golden rule applies even if we don't like the person. I had prayed to save Magpie, a year before when I knew my own death was only days away, and had seen the Kiowa with new eyes as a result. I could see that this was not a violent, hateful man before me, but an expression of the Great Spirit's idea, man. My prayers calmed me, and, opening my eyes, I felt the frantic atmosphere slipping away like a trout downstream.

I knew enough Comanche to tell his wife to hold him. Out of the crowd, a few other men joined her and, grasping the wounded man's limbs carefully, pinned him down. I didn't want to do more damage to the leg because he was thrashing about. Probing gently, I smelled the wound. There was nothing fetid yet, and it was still bleeding slowly—both good signs. The wound was relatively recent, I guessed. I made the hand gesture for water, and for fire. I needed to clean the area first and see how deeply the bullet was lodged.

A child brought me a leather pouch filled with water, but I needed something to boil it in. The black pots hanging over cookfires nearest me would never clean up quickly enough. I thought of using my copper pot, and, gesturing for everyone to stay, I ran for my tepee.

It took some gesticulating, but finally I got the cookpot safely to the side of the fire, and my copper pot filled with water. I washed my hands with an astringent root and rinsed them in the first pot, then ordered the child to bring me more water. I knew the Comanche must have thought I was insane, but I needed the time to collect myself and clean the wound. Next, I boiled my small knife as the children stared in fascination. The man lying on the buffalo robe had grown quiet, and as I fished my knife from the pot with the string I'd tied to its handle, I glanced back at him. Lovingly, the woman who had fetched me smoothed his face and hair, and I saw that he was as important to her as Johnny was to me.

As I knelt beside him, careful to keep my hands and knife free of any dirt, he asked my name. This time, he stared into my eyes. I replied in Kiowa, although I'd understood his Comanche.

"I am called Mythmaker, of Kicking Bird's clan."

My answer must have sunk in, for he laid his head wearily back into his woman's lap. Gesturing for the men to hold him tightly, I set to work, praying as I probed for the bullet. He must have passed out at one point; I felt him finally relax.

He never cursed me again. Even though he regained consciousness as I sprinkled the wound with golden-root, he kept his opinion to himself. His wife started to pull the buffalo robe over the wound, but I stopped her in time.

"No," I managed in Comanche, "air." The wound needed to breathe, but I couldn't say it. She nodded in comprehension, however, and I felt the muscles in the back of my neck relax.

Stretching as I rose, I smiled at her and at the men who'd served as assistants. The bullet hadn't cut any arteries, but on the bad side, it had been in there longer than I'd first thought. I couldn't answer their questioning look, but still I smiled and gestured for the men to lift him and carry him to his tepee. His wife, trailing behind the cadre of warriors, turned to give me a quick smile. If nothing horrible happened as a result of my ministrations, I had earned myself a friend. Nodding in return, I knelt to gather my herbs and wash my hands once more in the copper pot. Lifting it from its hook with the tail of my skirt, I felt other hands on mine. Women gathered around me, forcing my fingers free, chattering helpfully. I let them take the pot, and looked at the sky.

The gray day I'd been wallowing in only hours earlier had disappeared into a swirl of red and magenta, signaling a spectacular sunset. I wondered where the day had gone and realized I'd spent hours working on the shaman's leg. Wearily I turned for home, only to find my entourage following me. I gestured for them to dump the bucket of water, and ran for my tepee. I was exhausted and could not try to make conversation with any of them, knowing I would fall asleep in mid-sentence. Throwing myself into my tepee, I crawled under the buffalo robe. I never knew which women fed my fire or pulled the cover over my shoulders.

Chapter 6

The buffalo were gone for this season, and they all knew it. If they ever saw another buffalo on their traditional hunting grounds, it would be a sign from heaven, Johnny thought, that the white man would wither on the vine and die. Not likely, he mused, his rifle across his horse's withers. They'd be lucky to have rabbit in the fire tonight. Discouraged, he slammed the rifle in its scabbard. He'd find his companions and check out their luck. His long hair, grown since he'd cut it in mourning for his grandmother, lifted in the winter breeze. Nothing but his gray eyes betrayed his white blood, inherited from his soldier father. He wore the leather shirt and breechcloth, traditionally fringed and beaded, unlike the others dressed in a white man's shirt and hat. When he'd come home to the Comanche over a year ago to find Beth, he'd shed his last vestige of his life as an Army scout, burning his white man's clothes. He'd never been so free.

Winter would be hard this year. The Medicine Lodge Treaty was signed after he and Mythmaker crept from the camp, but he knew how the white man used his people. He'd been a sort-of white man long enough, scouting for the Army, to have a clear comprehension of what the treaty must have done to the Kiowa, the Cheyenne, the Arapaho, and the others foolish enough to think peace could be had by dipping a finger in ink and marking the white man's paper.

They had agreed, early that morning before setting out, to rendezvous at a stand of cottonwoods not far from where he paused now. The sun, no longer giving any warmth, sank quickly, and he pressed his heels to the ribs of his horse. This night would be hard for him. How quickly he'd become accustomed to the curve of Mythmaker's back pressed against his chest as they nestled together beneath the buffalo robe. He wondered how he could sleep without the scent of her near to him.

He no longer recognized the white woman, Elizabeth McFarland, in his wife, Mythmaker. Now and then, he remembered her as a child, when he and her brother would play in the dirt outside the post walls, poking frogs with sticks and shooting each other with imaginary guns. But from the moment he'd discovered her among the Kiowa, dressed in beaded leather, her hair smoothed with grease, her hands folded demurely on her knees as he entered the tent of her Kiowa grandfather, he'd seen only Mythmaker in her. As a half-Indian in the white man's world, he'd never have aspired to win her love. But as a Comanche warrior, he was worthy of her, and she returned his feelings. He considered himself blessed.

But her love wouldn't keep food in their stomachs. Sighing, he raised his eyes at the leaden, posttwilight sky, and prayed to find game. As though in answer to his petition, birds startled from their nightly roost in a stand of trees on the next rise. Quickly he pulled his rifle out again, wary. Food, friend, or foe, he would be ready.

Whatever was scattering the birds was either a serious predator or an immensely stupid human. The cacophony probably wouldn't have been noticed by a white man, but to Johnny, it was deafening. Carefully he dropped his horse's reins and slid to the ground. Darkness would give him needed cover, but with no moon, his ability to see his prey before being seen himself was questionable. Moving so that his scent wouldn't be carried by the night breeze, Johnny edged his way toward the trees.

Sniffing, he smelled white man before he saw him. What, he wondered, were the whites doing here? There was no army in the area, and he would have heard about settlers trying to cross into treaty lands. This one had built no fire, so whoever it was understood he was in danger on this land. Instinctively Johnny dropped to the ground, making himself invisible against the last of the winter sky. This must be one crazy white man, invading lands shrinking with every day the white man was in Comanche territory.

Lifting his head, Johnny absorbed the white man's odors again. No stink of dead buffalo, not enough oil to mean cleaned Army rifles, but plenty of fear. Whoever was under those trees was alone, and afraid of making a camp. For a second, Johnny considered going on his own way, meeting his companions, steering them away from this invader. But then he thought of Noble. What if he'd come after Johnny once more, in a final attempt to persuade Beth to return to her white life? As soon as he thought it, he knew Noble wouldn't come after them in this fearful way. No, this was someone who didn't belong on these lands, and who knew it. Johnny stopped thinking like a white man and slipped his knife from its sheath.

It was almost too easy to sneak up on the white man. Huddled under a saddle blanket, hat pulled deeply over his eyes, he chewed something from an opened saddlebag. Johnny could hear the man's mastications as clearly as he'd heard the angry chatter of the birds. Nearby, a hungry horse snuffled through the bed of dead leaves, searching for food. Reins tied to a log, the horse was one good-looking piece of flesh, and Johnny could see Mythmaker riding him proudly. Pushing the vision of his wife away, he set about his business.

He'd work his way behind the man, lash him to the tree against which he leaned, and find out, by whatever means necessary, what the man was doing on the treaty lands, before he killed him and took his horse. Slipping the leather belt from his waist, he crept behind the man. But he didn't have a chance to loop the belt around the man's throat, before the man jumped to his feet, Colt drawn, firing wildly into the darkness. With a piercing cry, Johnny lunged with his knife, slicing upward with a stroke not fatal but bloody enough to send the man to his knees clutching his chest.

Mercilessly Johnny shoved him facedown in the loam, kicking the gun toward the horse. Jerking the hat off, Johnny seized his hair in one hand, his knee in the small of the man's back like an anvil. Pricking the side of his white neck with the knife, Johnny spit out the words.

"What are you doing on Comanche lands, white man? Do you want to die?"

A gurgle of fear, strangled words in a constricted throat, was his only response. *"Ayiee,"* Johnny said and snorted in disgust as he rolled the man onto his back. What was such a coward doing in a place where he was sure to die?

The man's red hair glowed in the waning light, his skin pale with huge freckles, his face scarred by a long thin nose and eyes that were furious through his fear. Fingering the man's coat, Johnny knew for sure this was no Army man. He was a farmer, by the smell of him.

Slipping his rifle into the crook of his arm, Johnny sheathed the knife. This man was no threat, and killing him would be too easy. He'd take the horse and be done with the matter. Grunting, he rose to his feet. The white man clutched his chest.

"Won't kill you today, white man. But get off these lands, you want to keep that red hair." Twining the horse's reins in his hand, Johnny turned to leave.

The man's lunge surprised him. Hands around Johnny's throat, the man fought like a she-bear for her cubs. Breaking free, Johnny rolled away in astonishment not so much at the man's attack as at his own stupidity. He'd underestimated the stranger, and that gave him pause. Crouching, he drew his knife and, circling it in the air, he assessed the situation.

"You want to die, white man?" Johnny finally broke the stalemate, as the red-headed man glared at him from all fours, a shock of bright hair falling in his face. "You have no weapon, and I could kill you easily."

"You sure talk good," whispered the man through a fear-constricted throat. "You a white man gone Indian, or a savage?"

Snorting in derision, Johnny whistled for his horse. Crashing through the undergrowth, the horse stopped a few feet from Johnny. "Neither, fool. I offer you a chance to get away, and you try to kill me."

"You attacked me first!" The man's voice rose harshly, and Johnny sensed more than stupidity in the man's presence in Indian lands.

"You were lucky I wasn't feeling like killing tonight. Get out of here while you can." Briefly Johnny wondered why he spared this lone white man. Could it be because his lonely, vulnerable position in Indian lands reminded him of Noble?

"I'm staying. Until I get my wife back. Comanche, raided our farm week ago, Tuesday. Found her shoes, that was all."

His words explained a lot to Johnny. "She's dead, white man, if the Comanche took her. Used her long as they wanted, then killed her. Go home to your crops, get yourself another woman." Why hadn't he said the same words to Noble when he'd come asking for help to find Beth? The difference, he knew, was that he and Noble understood Beth and knew she'd fight to stay alive. What of this man's wife, was she of the same cut?

"She's not dead till I find her body, or someone who saw her die. Not you, not anyone, will make me believe her or her bones just vanished from this earth like that!" He snapped his fingers, rocking back on his heels as he did so.

Johnny considered his position. The man, by all rights, should be dead and his blood soaking into the ground, but something held him back. The man's hope, his belief in his wife, was as strong as a rope swung to a drowning man, and Johnny understood such feelings.

"Tell me your wife's name, exactly when you found her missing, what she looks like. I'll do some asking. But my price is that you go home, and wait for word. Tell me where to send any news." Johnny felt the fool. He knew he wouldn't even take the horse now.

Eagerly the man spilled out Hannah's name, her long blond hair, the mole at the bottom of her left earlobe. She'd worn her blue work dress that morning when he'd rode out, she'd been planning on doing the wash, for it was Monday, don't you see? He'd come home Tuesday to find her gone, the cabin burned, the sheets in the dirt. Hannah always was a tidy house-keeper, and she had her routine, she'd have done her laundry for sure.

Johnny heard the words rasping in the darkness.

"All right, I'll see what can be found out, stranger. Your name?"

"Harry, Harry Monroe. Leave word for me at Fort Arbuckle, I'm heading that way. Hear the Comanche been raiding down close to the border, figure I'll follow, see if I can find her there."

"I told you to go home!" Johnny cracked sharply.

Harry Monroe knew he had Johnny in the clutches of his own misery. "Fort Arbuckle, I said."

Grumbling, Johnny checked the sky for his bearings. He still had some traveling to do to find the cottonwoods and his companions, and nothing to show for today's hunt but one scared, stubborn white man he was about to let go. Sheathing his knife, Johnny trotted to the edge of the stand where he'd left his horse. Sharply he swung back to Monroe for a last word. The man's white skin shone like a peeled rabbit in the night.

"Take that horse, and ride him hard till you get your tail outta here, because I won't be able to save you from the men I'm with. Don't stop until you're as far south of here as that horse can carry you. I'll leave word at Fort Arbuckle."

Harry Monroe scrambled for the horse, panting hard with relief. "Thanks, stranger. What's your name, you mind my asking?"

Johnny thought for a second. His Comanche name would mean nothing to the man, and so he was reluctant to share it. "Johnny, Johnny Two Hats."

"Thank you for what you're doing. And for my life," he added lamely.

Johnny sensed this was a man who seldom gave

thanks, who believed he earned what he worked for. "Get riding," he muttered gruffly as he swatted the horse on the rump. He'd left the white man's world to find out who he really was, and he'd just discovered an unpleasant fact. When push came to shove, he couldn't entirely leave the white part of him behind.

Beth would understand. The thought stunned him like a solid fist in the gut. He wondered that he'd thought of her as Beth. Suddenly, he couldn't wait to get back to her, to reassure himself that his wife, Mythmaker, hadn't been taken over by the white woman who had been Beth McFarland.

His stomach grumbled, and he shook his head sadly. If they'd stayed in the whites' world, they wouldn't have gone hungry. It wasn't himself he was worried about, it was Mythmaker. Swinging onto his horse's back, he watched Harry Monroe, hunched in the saddle like a man who'd ridden too far for one day, lurch into the darkness.

There was no escape, he thought, not for him, not for Harry Monroe. The women they loved would never leave them, even in death.

Chapter 7

Cump Sherman and U.S. Grant stood on no formality. Sherman thought Grant would rue the day, if he already hadn't, that he'd agreed to run for president, and as for himself, he was head of the Army only because his old war friend had asked him to stay on and help him. Disdain for office gave the ginger-haired, steadily graying soldier certain privileged access to the Oval Office. Grant, rumpled, his tie pulled loose and crumbs from lunch on his vest, ran his rein-rough hands through his hair. Cump noticed the gray was beginning to be noticeable at the temples.

Sherman, ranking general of the Army, crazy as a fox, lounged in a leather chair, propped his booted foot across his knee, and chewed on a cigar. Washington's gloomy sky reflected little liveliness in the smaller office Grant used to actually try to work.

"Got one of those for me, Cump?" Grant gestured vaguely at the cigar.

"Thought you bought Havanas by the boatload

these days,'' teased Sherman. ''Here, have a real cigar, one that'll cure a raw throat and put some curl in your hair at the same time.''

The two West Pointers puffed contentedly in silence for a few minutes. Finally, Grant broke the stillness.

''Got any solution to the Indians yet, Cump? Texans are getting mighty upset with me. Doesn't look like that last treaty did much good.''

''You'd think Texas was some kind of mare, skittish at any dog howling in the night. Read the reports, sir, and I can't say as I believe half of them. If what they say is going on, there's a full-scale war down there, and those aborigines are winning it. Plain truth is, I'll believe half what I read if I see it with my own eyes, and that's the only time.''

''Interesting thought. Think they've exaggerated the atrocities, thinking I'll order the whole danged Army into Texas?''

''Makes sense. Kansas has been screaming so long, they got what they wanted. Texas figures it can outshout them.''

Grant swiveled to stare at the winter sky. ''So what do I tell them, Cump? Give me something to throw them, keep 'em happy. And it better not cost us any more lives.''

''Tell 'em Cump Sherman's coming. I'll ride on out, take a gander for myself. That oughta keep them happy, for a while.''

Grant turned again and peered at his old friend through a haze of cigar smoke. ''Be careful. Don't want to see that sorry skinny hair of yours separated from your head.''

Sherman harrumphed. "Don't believe all you read, General. I'd bet not one-fourth of the scalps those Texans claim got lifted came from heads in their neck of the woods. Think I'll travel light and fast, call on some of the posts along the border. They're the ones taking the brunt of things; they'll have a real picture for me."

Grant tapped the edge of the desk with his fingernail. "Don't get me into a mess I can't get out of without risking our boys, Cump. Folks are tired of killing, here in the East. Texas seems awful far away, and with Confederate sentiments."

"God Almighty, General, you're sounding like a politician!" exploded Sherman. "We're going to have to fight the tribes one of these days, and teach them a lesson like we did in Georgia. This pussyfooting around is what's getting us in trouble!"

Bristling, Grant straightened his shoulders, jabbing the cigar in the ashtray. "Please remember, this isn't the War, General, and there are some who see us as invaders in Indian lands. I must say, part of me agrees with them. I want this matter settled with a minimum of bloodshed on both sides. See to it."

Sherman understood he was being dismissed. "I'll send you reports as warranted, sir!" Saluting, he twirled on his heel. As he looked back, Grant's rumpled head was already bent over the desk, a small trail of smoke still rising from the cigar crumpled in the silver tray. He remembered when they both wore dirty, war-stained uniforms and cursed the day they knew they were better soldiers than anything else in life.

Sometimes, he wondered if Grant was still a soldier, and other times, he knew for sure.

Cump Sherman pulled on his cigar as he settled into his overcoat and hat. Already, his mind was in Texas.

Chapter 8

There was nothing I could do to help her and the other captives. I was surprised to see a grown white woman with the children, mostly Mexican, I guessed. The children made sense; they'd grow into tribal ways and become Comanche. But the woman's value lay only in trading her to the Army, and I didn't see this tribe as coming anywhere near an Army post. I couldn't exactly protect her, since I didn't yet have the position in this tribe that I'd held with the Kiowa, but I could see that she had food. In my first days as a captive, I'd almost starved to death, and this woman looked ready to eat vermin already.

I hadn't seen her in the spoils of the raid at first, I was so busy helping my patient. That night, exhausted by the events of the day and weary from sleeplessness without my husband, I finally sank into a deep dark place that went beyond slumber. Somewhere, at the end of a long tunnel, I knew a woman wept. In my dream, I assumed it was I who cried, but sensed it was someone else. Forcing myself to awaken, I lay in my tepee, my ears still in the tunnel of tears.

I heard it again and knew it wasn't a dream. I'd slept through the feasting, meager as it was, celebrating the return of the warriors. The steady drumming had served as a lullaby for me. Now, the crying slipped into sobs, and I drew my robe around me to search for its source. If it was a child, I would take it into my tepee for the night, sort it out tomorrow. Cruelty to children was unthinkable in a Comanche tribe, and I couldn't imagine why a child wept so forlornly, unless death had come into its family.

The cold bit my face as I poked out of my tepee. I wished, again, for my husband, then set out to follow my ears. Grasses grown brittle with winter snapped under my feet, but still, I could hear the weeping clearly. Circling behind the camp, I found myself near the offal pile. She was a pale bundle hunched on the ground, and as I grew closer, I could see, in the sliver of moonlight, she was no child, but a woman grown.

Her hair, pale as mine, draped her face, which was locked between her knees as she wept and rocked. Touching her shoulder, I instantly clapped my hand to her mouth. She stank.

"Hush," I whispered softly. "Are you hurt?"

I could see her eyes widen at my words. "Can't feel my feet, they're tied too tightly. Can you get me out of here?"

I shook my head, feeling for the thongs that bound her. "Who brought you here?" Her answer would give me a good idea of her ownership.

Shaking her head, she started to hiccup. "Those savages! My husband, he'll think I'm dead, he'll . . ."

Slipping my hand over the woman's mouth, I wondered how to tell her she'd have to learn how to survive this trial, and that if she couldn't, she'd die. "Stop thinking about your home. Do as you are told, work any job they give you, don't try to run, or you'll die. I'll loosen these bindings, but you must promise to do as I say, and I'll see what can be done for you."

She was so terrified, she didn't even ask me who I was, or why I spoke her language. I don't think she even knew I was a white woman once. Nodding her assent, she held up her hands.

Using the knife I'd used on the wounded man, I loosened the knots there, and at her ankles. Slipping my buffalo robe over her shoulders, I touched her head. "I was taken captive, by another tribe, and I survived. You can too, but you must decide you want to live."

I had no other words to help her. One of the men must have fancied her, for her to have survived this long. Johnny would have to undertake the proper negotiations to buy her from her owner. I, as a woman, had no authority to do so. Running back to my tepee, I huddled on my cold bed, missing my buffalo robe and my husband, unable to sleep once more. I hadn't asked the woman's name, and that fact bothered me. I'd once been nameless, faceless, a nonentity among the Kiowa. Had I become so inured to the harshness of life in the tribes that I was unwilling to attach an identity to one frightened white woman who probably wouldn't survive the week?

I knew I had a choice to make here, one that would affect both me and Johnny, as my husband. If I intervened for the woman, and Johnny lost stature because of me, I might have to leave the tribe, and him. Instantly, I knew that was not a possibility. Without Johnny, my life would be awash in shades of gray, so desolate I couldn't imagine going on. What if the woman was some worthless piece of work, not worth the time I'd already spent worrying about her? Yet, she had a husband. . . .

My mind must have twirled in circles until the sheer complexity of my dilemma shattered of its own weight. About dawn, as a pale sun crept up the winter sky, I knew I'd beaten this dead horse long enough, and I didn't know why I'd done so in the first place. There was only one thing I could do.

Lacing my moccasins, I stood outside my tepee. If I acted quickly, perhaps my husband wouldn't be blamed for my actions. Grabbing my bag of herbs, I headed for my patient first. Clearly, he was a man of authority and respect. If I could gain his ear, perhaps the risk would be less. I half listened for the woman's sobs, but she'd been quiet since I'd loosened her thongs. Perhaps my plan would work.

Now that the heat of battle with the wound was over, I was able to recognize the tepee I visited. His wife, an older woman of immense dignity and with gray in her hair, rocked on her haunches over the cooking fire set outside her home. Kneeling beside her, I rested on my heels. Haltingly I asked, half in Comanche, half in sign language, how her husband had slept.

Shaking her head, she conveyed sparingly that it had been a hard night. Pointing to my bag of herbs, I asked if I could see him. She hesitated a second. I gestured as though I scooped food from the pot, and tried to say that he could not eat me for breakfast. Laughing, she rose, and held back the door for me.

I could see why she was concerned. The pain of the wound must have been ferocious, but the only sign was a deep line drawn across the man's forehead and lips pale with the hurt. His eyes, shut but not in sleep, flew open at my touch on his hand. Again, I used the word for permission and pointed to the leg. The pain clouding his eyes couldn't mask that this was a man of authority. Imperceptibly he nodded.

The wound was just about where I'd thought it would be, angry and red, but, thank goodness, without any telltale red lines radiating outward. It smelled clean, and I thought I saw evidence that it was starting to draw. I needed to clean away the drainage from last night, but I knew it would be even more painful than my surgery yesterday. Again, I made the gesture for water and pointed at the leg.

He nodded once more, his face less gray now that he understood my purpose. His wife ducked out and returned this time with someone else's copper pot, filled with water that was already warm. I smiled my thanks.

"This will cause you pain," I offered in Kiowa, hoping he understood some of the language. "I will mix you a drink first, and you may sleep." Pulling my herbs from their leather pouch, I held my hands to my lips and pretended to drink, then rested my head on my palm and made a snoring noise.

My actions pulled a ghost of a smile from him. But he wasn't buying it, and shook his head in the negative. "Do it," he ordered, then reached for the edge of the buffalo robe and held on tightly.

Dipping my precious supply of clean cloth in the pot, I wrung it out and began to dab gently around the edges of the hole. His leg never moved, and only the visible clenching of his hands gave away the pain. Once I'd cleaned away the last of it, I pronounced myself satisfied. "Hungry?" I asked my patient, rubbing my stomach.

His black eyes never left my face as I worked. I'd felt them burning into my skin, now into my eyes. He nodded slowly, and I turned to find his wife just behind me. I gestured as though drinking from a bowl and pointed at her husband.

Smiling, she disappeared, reappearing with an old-fashioned gourd with a long neck. I saw, as she handed it to me, that it had been hollowed and now held some sort of broth. Slipping my hand under my patient's head, I lifted him slightly, spilling some of the soup as I put his lips to the edge. He took a sip and grimaced. I forced the gourd to his lips once more. Obediently he drank again.

This time my eyes met those of his wife. Crinkling at the corners, they smiled into mine, and without words, we agreed that men were like children when they were sick or injured, and what was a woman to do but baby them? What was a woman to do?

Why am I taking such pains with this man? I

watched him working to swallow and knew that, no matter what he'd done, I'd have helped him. But now I had a reason beyond my conscience. I used the word for white woman, and pointed to my hair. "There," I gestured, meaning not me, but outside. I could tell by his eyes that he understood.

"Do you have right to her?" I could use the Kiowa phrasing, which meant a woman in the grass, which meant he'd used her, and had the right to do so any-time, but the words in Comanche were beyond me. Again, his eyes blinked. I glanced at his wife and saw confusion. It was understandable; she'd been busy with him, but this must have come as something of a surprise. I didn't think, watching her, that it was a pleasant one.

Barely nodding, his face grew wary.

"She weeps," I gestured to imaginary tears on my cheeks. "I would trade for her, and give you respite from her tears." I used the sign language for trade, and woman. "A gift, for my husband," I added for-mally, pretending submission to my husband.

I could see he was mulling over what he thought I'd said. Probably, I hadn't made myself clear. Bar-gaining with a man in pain is never a good idea, I reminded myself. I'd have to put it off for another day, I decided as he didn't answer me. Gathering my herbs back into their pouches, I gestured that I would take my farewell.

His wife followed me out, nodding her thanks. I saw her glance in the direction I'd gestured for the white woman, doubt in her eyes.

"Come," I ordered. Now I knew the correct tack

to take. We women could move mountains, if we worked together. Leading the way, I led her to where the woman huddled under my buffalo robe.

"I've brought someone who can help you, if she will," I began unceremoniously.

The woman flipped her matted hair from her face and raised her tear-reddened cheeks. "I'm so hungry," she moaned.

"Listen to me, I will find you food, but you must impress upon this woman that you are going to be a threat to her, that you will sleep with her husband every chance you get. Now, smile."

I was pleased with the alacrity with which she obeyed. Her face, though dirty, could have been pleasing if misery hadn't slapped her around so much, I thought. Turning to the warrior's wife, I shrugged. She had the power to make her husband's life miserable if she didn't like the white woman in her tepee, and she and I both knew it.

"I will help you," I began slowly. "Help me."

I knew she understood, as she placed a hand on the white woman's shoulder and forced her to rise. Pointing to me, she ordered the woman to go with me. Uncertain, her feet still bound, the woman took an unceremonious hop toward me.

"*Aagh,*" my newfound friend spat in disgust. Pulling her knife from her waist sheath, she sliced at the leathers. Giving the woman a shove, she again ordered her to follow me.

"Your husband?" I inquired gently.

I gathered from her reply that she'd take care of

him. Reaching for her work-worn hand, I squeezed it in friendship. There would be no debt between us.

"What is your name?" I asked quietly in English as the woman trailed me back to my tent.

"Hannah. Hannah Monroe," she mumbled. "And please, can I have something to eat?"

"Well, Hannah, I'll feed you what I've got, but you're about to learn your second lesson of Indian life. An empty belly is the normal state of things, this time of year. Now make sure you keep your distance. I want the others to think I own you, you understand?"

I was sure she didn't, but she'd learn if she wanted to survive. When Johnny got back, we'd figure out between us what to do with her. *Just what I need,* I thought and shook my head as I slid into my tepee, another woman in the same room with me and my husband. No wonder the wife was so eager to be rid of her. I understood completely.

Chapter 9

He was so glad to be home, to be back with Myth-maker, he could barely contain himself. They had never been separated since their first night together, and this hunting party had been out longer than he liked. But game had been scarce, and no one wanted to quit until there was something to show for all their work.

He saw her back first, as she bent over something in her lap. Her blond hair shone like a star, and he was drawn to her, to the great amusement of his friends, who saw his hunger and knew it wasn't for food.

"Wife!" he called to her, cupping his hand to make sure the sound flowed in her direction. He saw her head come up as though she heard him, but she merely rubbed the back of her neck as though it ached, and bent back to her task.

He was slightly annoyed. "Mythmaker!" he tried this time, wondering if perhaps she thought some other man called to his woman. Still, she ignored him. More than annoyed, he jumped from his horse's back, and landing on pins in his feet, strode to her side.

"Wife, I call you. I have missed you," he added softly, his hand on her shoulder.

The frightened face turned up to his wasn't Mythmaker's. Stunned, he stumbled back a step, wondering who wore her dress, and why, and where did this white woman come from. In English, he tried again, hoping she wasn't a Swede or German with no language he possessed.

"Where is my wife, woman? The blond-hair, the one whose clothing you wear?"

The woman struggled, emotions flying across her eyes faster than a tornado. "I don't know for sure. She is gone for the morning." Her voice was low, as though she were unaccustomed to speaking. "She gave me this dress," she added lamely, as though an explanation were in order.

Johnny could only wonder what Mythmaker had been up to in his absence. The woman looked pinched, but otherwise in good shape. Refusing to look at Johnny, she stared at the leather in her lap that she'd been working.

"How did you get here?" He decided the direct approach was best. Mythmaker was probably out hunting herbs or tending someone who was ill and he'd get answers faster from the woman herself anyway.

"Some of the men in this camp, they stole me from our ranch. I"—she choked on the words—"I thought I was going to die. The white woman saved my life. She has said . . ." The woman paused, as though she'd said too much already. Stiffening her shoulders, she continued, ". . . that she too was a captive once."

Johnny grumbled. It was just like his wife to stick her fingers into someone else's stewpot, and stir it up. It was natural, of course, that Mythmaker should empathize with this woman, but why did she have to take her under her wing? Johnny realized the white woman must have been plunder, and he wondered what Mythmaker had traded to get her. He shuddered involuntarily. His wife was no longer with the Kiowa, and though they'd been with his tribe almost a year now, she had yet to attain the same status she'd held with Kicking Bird's tribe.

"Which direction?" He touched the woman's shoulder again, upset that she stared at her lap as he spoke to her. What did she think, that he was going to ravish her on the spot? "Where did my wife go when she left?" he continued.

She pointed west, toward the river. Tying his horse to the stake outside his tepee, he smoothed back his long hair with both hands as he strode forcefully to find Mythmaker. Slight annoyance at finding another mouth to feed was tempered by his happiness to be home. Mythmaker, he told himself, would have a plan for what to do with the white woman. He just hoped it didn't involve his riding into the nearest Army post with her. With Colonel McFarland back East, and Noble, Mythmaker's brother, nowhere he knew of, it would be hard to prove his innocence in the capture of this white woman. What a nuisance! He sighed as once more he smoothed his hair, hoping to find his wife alone.

Reaching the riverbank, he shivered in the wind rising off the water. He'd have to trade for furs to make his wife a warmer coat this season. She was so thin, he knew this winter would cut her to the bone. For a brief second, he felt guilty at taking her from a warm white man's house, where she could have sat by her father's hearth and eaten her fill any time she desired. But he knew that was not her way; she'd chosen him, and the life they now led.

His heart was overflowing with joy that she'd chosen him to love. "Mythmaker! Wife!" he called to her, hoping she'd find him before he had to traipse up and down the riverbank to find her. He glimpsed a motion to his left and trotted toward it.

She rocked back and forth on her knees, her hair bound in leather, grunting. With a shout, she hurled something green into the basket by her side. Twisting to settle the stuff deeper in the straw, she shouted in surprise.

"You! You are back!" Tumbling to her feet, she spilled into his arms, oblivious to her basket. "I've missed you, husband," she whispered, trying to appear demure.

"And I you!" he thrilled, swinging her in his arms, as though she were a child.

Finally, he set her on her feet as she tried to smooth her dress and hair. "We are too old to act like such children!" she laughed, glancing around to see if they'd been overheard.

"Huh!" He was unrepentant. Bending, he replaced her scattered weeds in her basket. "And what have you found now?"

"Some wild onions, a last bit of mint, and tubers I believe we can boil and eat! I have been very productive this morning, husband!" She thrilled every time she called him "husband."

"Did you think the hunt would be so unsuccessful?" he teased. He didn't dare tell her the truth, that the game was scarce and scattered, and it had taken much longer than any of them had expected to come up with meat.

Glancing at the sky, she shivered. "Snow soon. Won't be able to gather much, once the ground's covered."

He knew by her answer that she understood the trouble they'd had with the hunt. Gathering her into his arms, he hugged her close, rejoicing in the feel of her heart next to his. He never thought of her as a white woman anymore, just as the most precious person in the world.

"Come, let's get back. I'm hungry, and I want to show you what I've brought." Taking her basket, he knew he was violating the warrior's picture of himself by helping her with women's work. But the tribe understood that some white ways clung to him, even if not to her. Taking her hand in his, he led the way back up the riverbank. A leaden gray sky hovered above them, and he felt a raindrop on the back of his hand.

"Hurry, we'll get wet!" Laughing, Mythmaker raced beside him. He was so eager to get home with her, he forgot about the white woman outside his tepee.

Scuttling into the tepee after his wife, he stopped in

shock. The white woman knelt before the fire, feeding it slowly.

Mythmaker paused in the midst of lifting her plunder from the basket. "Hannah, have you met my husband?" She frowned at Johnny's reaction.

"Yes," the woman answered softly.

The name registered slowly with Johnny. Monroe, the white man on a fool's mission, had said his wife's name was Hannah. Groaning, Johnny asked her last name, in English.

"Monroe," she replied, even more softly.

Why had the gods done this to him? He never expected to actually find Harry Monroe's wife. "Is your husband thin, with red hair?"

Her face brightened as she stared forthrightly into his. "Yes, yes, have you seen him? Is he alive?"

Numbly Johnny nodded. Speaking in Kiowa to his wife, he asked, "How long has she been here? Where did you get her?"

Mythmaker answered in kind, her face alert. "The tall fierce one, left before you with a raiding party. Came back wounded, I tended to him. His wife and I, we arranged the trade, my services for the white woman. I have kept her here with me. She has not been used poorly since she came to the camp."

He knew Mythmaker understood why he asked.

"Mister, where did you see him, my husband! You gotta tell me!" Hannah Monroe crawled over to Johnny and clung to his arm.

He felt her fingers biting through the leather of his shirt.

"He was many days' ride from here, woman.

Searching for you.'' He could only tell her the truth, although he had no great hopes that the foolish Harry Monroe was still alive.

"Got to find him! Got to get home!'' Her face aglow, the white woman shoved for the doorway.

Mythmaker grabbed her by the shoulders. ''Don't be a fool. You can't walk out of here, like one of the tribe. They've allowed you to stay with me, because of Johnny's prestige within the tribe. You start running, they'll fill your back full of arrows so fast you'll see God before your next breath.''

She queried him in Kiowa. ''Do you think the husband is alive? How did you find him?''

''I tried to kill him,'' Johnny answered simply. ''But I couldn't. Told him I'd leave word at Fort Arbuckle, if I heard where his wife was.'' He suppressed the oath he wanted to shout. In making the promise to Harry Monroe, he never thought he'd have to honor it. He'd assumed that the man's wife was long dead.

Mythmaker searched in her white memory for Fort Arbuckle. ''How are you going to do this thing you've promised?'' She understood completely that Johnny never reneged on a promise. He'd promised to find her, and he had.

''I never said when. Weather coming like this, I can't travel fast, and I won't leave you alone. It'll have to wait,'' he decided unilaterally.

His wife narrowed her eyes and stared at the white woman, sobbing gently into her fists. ''We'll all drown in her tears, if you wait too long.''

Johnny could do nothing but laugh. Mythmaker had sounded just then like a proper Comanche wife. ''You got us into this, my wife. Think of another solution, let me know.''

Rolling her eyes, Mythmaker shook her head. They both knew they couldn't cast her off or trade her to another warrior. Hannah Monroe was to be their burden, for however long it took to reunite her with her husband. Johnny knew there'd be other, bigger problems than Mrs. Monroe's for them to face before this winter was over. Mythmaker handed him a bowl filled with the stew she'd been brewing over the fire outside. Dipping his hand in, Johnny savored the smell of herbs and plants Mythmaker used to enliven their plain fare. They had very little, but she made everything better. The thought of their meager possessions reminded him of the last council he'd attended.

''We move the camp in two days' time, I forgot to tell you.'' He chewed slowly as he spoke. ''To the Washita. The Cheyenne have left their reservation, and there will be many of us there, along with our allies. There will be protection for us in greater numbers, as well.''

Mythmaker nodded solemnly, handing Hannah a bowl of stew. In a true Comanche household, Hannah would be doing all the heavy work, as well as serving her masters. The white woman would never know what she'd escaped. ''Will there by any Kiowa? Any of my clan?'' How she longed to see Grandfather, Magpie.

Johnny shrugged. ''Don't know. Most probably.'' For a second, he wondered if his wife would want to return to her people for an extended visit. It happened in his tribe, when a woman missed her people so much she dragged her lower lip on the ground, a misery to all who saw her. If she did, he'd have to go with her. He couldn't bear to be without her.

As though she could read his thoughts, she pressed a hand to his cheek. "Don't worry, husband. My home is with you."

Almost as if she understood Mythmaker's words, Hannah Monroe burst into an even heavier spate of tears. Rolling her eyes, Mythmaker moved beside the woman and put a comforting arm around her. Her eyes told Johnny that she was sorry she'd dragged him into such a mess.

Chapter 10

General William T. Sherman chose the chore himself. He wanted his words to Sheridan to be clear to his old comrade. Sheridan, for all his diminutive size and bantam attitude, was a stickler for detail, and Sherman wanted him unequivocally empowered about the extent of his authority. He drafted the order in longhand, and only after letting it sit for a day so he could reflect upon the wording did he hand it to his secretary to make an official copy. He and Sheridan had discussed the campaign in detail. Hazen would take the southern reservations and ostensibly protect the innocent among the tribes who stayed on their treaty lands. No mercy was to be shown to those whose noses Hazen hadn't counted among his charges. Sheridan would make war on those who roamed and still believed themselves free men, as they'd never been warred upon before.

Despite his predilection for total warfare, Sherman felt a passing pity for the hostiles who thought they could defy the U.S. Government and its treaties. They had no idea whom they were dealing with, but they would soon learn.

Sheridan's orders were complete and unequivocal. "Go ahead your own way and I will back you with my whole authority," Sherman wrote to Sheridan. "If it results in the utter annihilation of these Indians, it is but the result of what they have been warned again and again. . . . I will say nothing and do nothing to restrain our troops from doing what they deem proper on the spot, and will allow no mere vague general charges of cruelty and inhumanity to tie their hands, but will use all the powers confided to me to the end that these Indians, the enemies of our race and of our civilization, shall not again be able to begin and carry out their barbarous warfare on any kind of pretext they may choose to allege."

Chapter 11

The Cheyenne camped along the banks of the Washita River huddled in their tepees, sound asleep and not
eager to greet another cold winter morning. Their allies, the Arapaho, Kiowa and Comanche, spread their
villages beside the same water for some fifteen miles,
all content with a winter camp so early in the season.
Winter meant meager supplies as the game was hunted
out, but it also had a life-saving quality greatly antic-
ipated by the tribes. When the snows flew, they were
safe from the yellow-legs, the cavalrymen who hunted
them like dogs. They were tired of running, and Black
Kettle's camp was known for its leader's refusal to
take up the war lance against the whites. His pacifism
and the weather would serve as an adequate protection.

A baby cried for its breakfast, and as its mother
rolled over to feed it, the father stepped from the tepee
to make water. Stretching, he contemplated returning
to his blankets, when he heard the noise. The noise

became a sort of music, strange and discordant to his ears. Although he had no idea who was playing, he recognized the white man's instrument, the trumpet, as the source of the music. A quick tune, the sound grew louder by the second, until the man remembered where he'd heard such an instrument before. In the mouth of a yellow-legs, it signaled an attack. Shouting, he dove for his weapons, roughly shoving his wife into the cold, their child at her breast.

"Run!" he screamed. "To the river. Stay hidden!"

She thought he'd lost his mind, until she too heard the sound. Staring in the direction from which it wafted in the thin morning air, she paused only long enough to know the ground trembled with the hooves of many horses, and that she would die if she stayed with her husband. Screaming for her family members in other tepees, she tried to rouse as many as possible before sliding down the banks of the river. Slipping her baby into the bodice of her leather gown, she ignored his hungry wails, and ran as fast as she could through the shallow edge of the river, oblivious to the cold that stung her skin and froze her feet.

Yellow-hair Custer had been unleashed against the Cheyenne. When his Osage scouts came across the fifty-one tepees of the Cheyenne village on the Washita River, the short hairs on the back of his neck stood on end, and it wasn't the cold that caused the reaction. Sheridan had given him carte blanche, and his platter was full before him. He was to exterminate the Indians, destroy their tepees, their supplies, and their horses. He was good at this job, and he knew it. The wintery dawn was split like seasoned wood with the bugles blowing ''Gary Owen'' until the spit in them froze, and all that was left to do was kill.

As the woman scuttled down the water's edge, she saw the bluecoats upon her village like so many ants. She gathered other women and children to her, all of them wild-eyed and determined. Most half-dressed, feet freezing in the water, they were oblivious to the cold as they sought to hide from every clatter of rifle fire; they could hear the shouts of their men as they fought to defend their homes. The woman, holding her baby under her dress as she ran, discerned from the rapidity of the bluecoats' assault that there was little hope for her people, most of them still asleep in their beds. The woman knew that if she ran fast enough, she could rouse their allies, camped farther down the river, and perhaps there was hope. But only if she moved quickly. She couldn't do so along the river's edge, and suddenly, she decided she had to reach the upper bank once more. Thrusting her baby into the arms of another young woman who ran beside her, she scrambled up the rocky bank.

A quick glance at her village told her she had better run like she'd never run before. Bluecoats swarmed their tepees like angry wasps, and the steady rat-a-tat-tat of their weapons never ceased. Tears blinding her eyes, she ran through the ice and snow until she thought her heart would crack open and bleed against her skin. She knew her husband was dead, and that her people, Black Kettle's Cheyenne, didn't have much more time before they entered the spirit world.

Her blood thumped so loudly in her ears, she no longer heard the soldiers firing, or the snow-muffled hooves behind her. As something grabbed her flying hair, she thought at first a raven must be plucking her from earth, a special raven sent by the gods to carry her quickly on its back to the tepees of the Kiowa and Comanche. Raising her arms to be carried aloft, she halfturned and saw the bluecoat, the sun on silver in his hand, and still, she wondered where her friend the raven had gone. Before she could ask her question, the blue-coated arm swung down into her neck with the silver saber, and she felt no pain, only surprise that she had been so wrong.

The slaughter continued most of the morning. Custer looted the tepees for the best shields and lances, beaded clothing, and quivers. As his soldiers shot the Cheyenne's horse herd, he ordered the torching of the winter supplies of pemmican. Lieutenant Godfrey, after finishing his chore with the horses, followed the trail of the Cheyenne who had escaped along the east ridge line. Galloping to a hill about two miles from the village, he halted his platoon with a hand frozen not just with the cold. As far as he could see, tepees carpeted the valley, and around them flew circles of Indians with weapons raised. He knew what it meant. Racing back to Custer, he reported that he'd been seen, and had had to cover his retreat back to the Cheyenne village.

Custer was tempted with the thought of more victory. But ammunition was running low, and he was anxious to get his prisoners and word of his stunning success back to headquarters. Lieutenant Elliott hadn't yet returned, but Custer was itchy around the ends of his mustache at the thought that perhaps his wagon train, inadequately guarded on the banks of the Canadian River, might be found by the tribes. Lieutenant Bell had come through with the ammunition when it was needed, but the men's overcoats and haversacks, left in the snow when the charge came, had been lost. The temperature was dropping rapidly. It was time to get the devil out of there. Custer had always obeyed his instincts, and this time was no exception.

Moving east, as though to attack the other villages found by Lieutenant Godfrey, Custer scattered the Indians. Night was falling fast, and they had planned an ambush that was foiled by Custer's feint. Returning to the ruins of Black Kettle's camp, the tribesmen stared in horror at the snow drenched in blood, great trails of it in all directions in which the shot horses had run, bleeding from the soldiers' bullets. There was nothing they could do to save the horses, or the Cheyenne captives being driven through the snow with the bluecoats.

The Cheyenne women and children huddled under meager blankets or perched, one bare foot up, then the other, in the snow of Camp Supply. Their faces bore the mark of weariness more than sorrow, as though the march from the Washita had taken the last of their strength. The soldiers had shot their horses, their pride as well as their transportation. Their men and families lay unburied in the snow beside their burning tepees. They had much to bear, but not a one wailed or wept.

That night Custer and some of his men took their pick from among the Cheyenne women. One of them, nine moons later, bore a son, whom she named after his father, the yellow-hair.

Custer had obeyed Sheridan's orders. The Plains Indians would now experience total warfare such as they'd never seen coming from the white men.

Chapter 12

We were late to the banks of the Washita. In the melee that followed the slaughter of Black Kettle's people, the other tribes had early that afternoon gathered their men and weapons and ridden to the Cheyenne camp. They were in time only to see the ashes of the proud Cheyenne possessions, to stare in shock at the tumble of bodies and the slain horses. To a Comanche, killing a horse is worse than killing a human being.

Johnny told me about it, that the banks were now called "Red Moon," for the blood that had soaked the snow in the moonlight. I had gone to the Kiowa to search for Magpie and Grandfather, and returned late to find my husband sitting by our fire, his face streaked with ashes. But I am getting ahead of myself, and must in fairness tell the happy with the sad.

Kicking Bird's people had come to the Washita, and I dared not hope that Grandfather was with them still. He was an old man when I came to the people, and the year since had been hard for all of us. I know it may sound trite, but I cannot describe how my heart filled to bursting with joy as I saw him leaning in his rawhide chair against the side of the tepee, sunning himself in the wan winter light! Ignoring the calls of my friends and former patients, I had eyes only for him.

"Grandfather," I began formally, "it is I, your daughter, returned for a visit." I was careful to maintain the formalities.

Opening one eye in his leathered face, the old chief gave me a deliberate nod. "It is good, Daughter, to see you again. How fares your husband?"

I had had enough of the proper etiquette, and seized his worn hands in mine, tears freezing on my cheeks. "It is well, Grandfather, it is well. I miss my people and Magpie, and you, but it is well."

It felt wonderful to be understood, to not have to prove myself. I refrained from helping him as he lumbered to his feet. I knew he was still a proud man though I could see that the arthritis was beginning to bother him more than he would tell me.

"Come, Daughter, warm yourself by the fire," he invited simply as he held aside the flap for me. I demurred, as was proper, and gestured that I would follow him inside. Age commands great respect among the Kiowa, especially for a chief who had been as great in his youth as Grandfather. When I had saved the life of Magpie, a lifetime ago for me, he had seemed to me to be a man of formidable power and barely suppressed anger. When we wept together with joy at the life restored to his grandson's body, I had seen a soul kindred to mine.

I rejoiced to be in my old home again. How often through the winter nights had I traced letters for Magpie, using berries collected in the fall for ink. Kneeling on the appropriate side of the fire, I waited for my grandfather to tell me his news. Most of all, I wanted to see Magpie.

As was proper, he lit his pipe, using the correct and, to me, infinitely slow rituals. He would smoke as we chatted, and even today I can smell the ghost of that pipe. He even deigned to gossip a bit with me, in between a recitation of the tribe's travels since the banks of the Medicine Lodge. I heard who had returned from raids having counted coups, who had produced more children, and the stories of the white eyes who killed the land by their slaughter of the buffalo. Finally, I could stand it no longer.

"Grandfather," I burst out, like a child who can no longer wait for Father Christmas, "where is Magpie? I would like to see him!"

Grandfather smoothed his hair back and rolled his powerful shoulders into a hunch. I caught my breath, afraid to hear the answer to the question I had asked.

"I have sent him, my daughter, to our cousins the Arapaho, to learn what he must to be a great chief. The more he understands of all our people, the greater he will become."

I could see the sadness and defiance in his eyes.

Once, I had convinced him that Magpie must learn the ways of the whites if he was to lead his people into a peaceful coexistence with them. Clearly, my absence had changed the picture.

"You did what you thought best, Grandfather," I answered tactfully. "I wish I could have stayed, to continue Magpie's lessons."

"It was not your fault, Daughter, that you had to flee the soldiers who would have taken you from us, at the treaty grounds. But Magpie grows quickly and soon will be a young man. If he does not understand the old ways, how can he teach our people the new?"

I knew then that the old man was wiser than I. I just hoped Magpie was somewhere near. "Could a message be sent to him, Grandfather, that I would like to visit?"

Smiling gently, Grandfather reached for my hand across the side of the fire. "I have already done so, as soon as I heard that your husband's people were coming to join us in winter camp. He should be here soon."

I could barely contain my joy. Someday, I believed back then, I might have a child of my own to love and praise, but Magpie was my firstborn, even though he didn't come from my body.

"Go, Mythmaker, and visit your old friends. I will see that Magpie comes to you, as soon as he arrives." Grandfather knew I would have a difficult time sitting still, until I saw Magpie.

Gratefully I accepted his advice. I was greeted with general joy and thanksgiving, and made to feel welcome wherever I scratched at a door. I could see that my people were doing well, and their preparations for winter were more complete than my own. But still, there was a general unease that worried me. Finally, after talking with enough women, I knew what it was.

The Medicine Lodge Treaty was not going to work. The Kiowa were still driven by the need to raid, and to roam to find buffalo. The women understood, better than the men, the cost of disregarding the treaty. They knew there would be many moons of aching, hungry stomachs for their children, and of wailing for the men who never returned from fights with the bluecoats. The white men were never far from their thoughts, and because they no longer saw the white in me, I heard their fears.

I was beginning to sink from my previous elation at coming home, when I turned to see a familiar figure striding quickly between the lodges. But something was wrong, and I wasn't sure what. Before I could put my finger on it, I was enveloped in a huge hug, squeezing the air from my body. I could hardly believe that the small arms I'd once cradled were now capable of spanning me so easily. A year is a long time in the life of a young boy.

"Mythmaker!" he shouted, heedless of any proprieties. I struggled in his arms, knowing his size was what was wrong about him.

"Release me, boy!" I scolded playfully, tugging at his hair. His face lit up like a full moon as he danced around me like the child he clearly was leaving behind. "What will everyone think, their shaman acting so silly!"

Immediately, he put on a serious expression, though I could tell it was difficult for him, and pretended to age twenty years.

"Greetings, Shaman, and welcome to our village," he intoned solemnly. I almost laughed as his voice cracked in midsentence.

"Pshaw, stop this nonsense!" Grabbing his paw in my hand, I wondered if he would be like a puppy, and grow into the current size of his extremities. "Come home and tell me all about what you have learned among the Arapaho," I began as I tugged him in the direction of Grandfather's tepee.

Oblivious to all except my own happiness in being once again with my Kiowa family, I didn't immediately notice the man running into the camp. Vaguely, I heard cries of "Eonah-pah" and shouts of alarm.

Stopping like a stone in my path, Magpie's boy-man face froze as he heard more than I. Perhaps I just didn't want to hear what the man, clearly distressed, was shouting.

"Come, we must see what has happened," Magpie urged as I trotted away from him, toward Grandfather's lodge. Apprehension iced down my back at the growing body of shouts, and horror on the faces that surrounded Eonah-pah. I knew him to be a seasoned warrior and remembered a friendly man. Magpie continued to tug at my hand, and ultimately I gave in.

I will never forget the chilling tale told by Eonah-pah that afternoon. His words were colder than a bird-killing winter. Practically shouting, he told how the bluecoats, so many they outnumbered all the Cheyenne of Black Kettle's camp by four to one, cut down the people, women and children included, in a dawn attack. A visitor among the Cheyenne, he had grabbed his bow and quiver of arrows, and run to protect the women and children fleeing along the riverbanks. He'd evaded a saber-wielding trooper and stabbed his horse so that the women could gain some time and distance. As he spoke, I could hear the women screaming, the dogs howling, the shouts of the men as they fought with bows and arrows amid a hail of bullets.

Eonah-pah had seized a quiver from the dead chief, Little Rock, and continued firing until he could find shelter in a line of timber. From there, he'd made his way as quickly as he could to his own people, to sound the alarm. He had seen some Arapaho joining some Cheyenne from other camps in the timbers, and wished to rejoin the battle as soon as he was rearmed and horsed.

I knew Magpie was still too young, and Grandfather too old, to join the fight. But my husband wasn't. I knew, as I stared at the stricken faces surrounding Eonah-pah, that as I had joyed in seeing my people, the Kiowa, again, my husband was already facing death.

Falling to my knees in the snow, I wrapped my face in my hands. I didn't want to hear his war cry, see his death, but the image moved across my eyes involuntarily.

"Magpie, I must return to my husband's lodge now. Please tell Grandfather I will come again, if and when I can. I love you."

With those words, I fled. I didn't care about anything, except seeing my husband once more before he died.

Chapter 13

I waited through the long night for my husband's return. Hannah cowered in a corner of my tepee, her eyes wide when I told her the soldiers were killing farther downriver. At first, she thought she could run to them and be saved, but I pointed out, none too gently, that they'd shoot her before they realized she was white. After a few protests, she saw the wisdom of my words. I didn't tell her that she'd be killed before she could flee the village, especially if anyone thought the soldiers were heading to the Comanche settlement.

I sat by my fire all night, tending it slowly, not allowing myself to think the worst. Johnny was cool-headed and could talk sense into a charging buffalo. But what I'd heard from the women who came to scratch at my door and whisper the latest news of the slaughter on the Washita, was so horrifying, there would be no ears to hear common sense.

To occupy myself, I began to pack. No matter what

happened, I knew that winter camp for the People was finished in this place. The ghosts of the dead would come to haunt us. I had no idea where we would go, or if we would stay with the Noconee, or return to Kicking Bird's camp. No matter what, I knew we were not safe in this place.

Throughout the night, survivors of the Washita drifted into our camp. I could hear the women wailing, and knew that I would have many patients among those who would let the white shaman touch them. I must admit, my confidence in my position in the tribe began to erode with each passing hour. Among my own people, the Kiowa, I was never aught but one of the People. But here, with Noconee Comanche, I was a white woman with healing arts, married to a half-breed.

I will never forget the dawn when my husband returned, safely, to our home. Although horror and bone-weariness were in his face, his eyes for me were nothing short of loving. Rising to greet him, I wrapped my arms about his cold shoulders and held him to me as tightly as I could. He buried his face in my hair, and I could feel the shuddering breaths he took as he absorbed my scent. Seeing Hannah in her corner, he released me and sat by the fire so quickly, I wondered what was wrong.

Raising his light-colored eyes to mine, he could not conceal from me the burning anger within them. Chilled by the hatred I saw, I pulled my robe closer and knelt, entirely improperly, beside him at the fire. He didn't notice my lack of manners. Pulling his cold hands into mine, I was shocked that his felt more chilled than mine. I began chaffing them between my palms, waiting for him to tell me what must be said.

"All we found were bodies. Everything burned. Even the children's toys." His eyes said what the words didn't. He spoke in English, and I knew he did so for Hannah's sake. He wanted her to understand that what she'd experienced was nothing compared to what he'd seen that day.

"But I thought the Cheyenne who wintered here were friendly with the whites?" I was having trouble understanding what was happening. The Army didn't campaign in the winter, and I, more than anyone, as the daughter of an Army officer, understood this. I also knew the Army was careful to attack only those who deserved punishment. This didn't sound like my father's army.

"Black Kettle, yes, he was. Didn't save him, though. Tried to escape on horseback, his wife up behind him. Both dead. Even the whites who were part of the tribe were shot! I saw it, with my own eyes!" His anguish was heart-wrenching. My husband had served the Army for many years as a scout, he'd grown up in shadows of Army posts, with his Indian mother following his soldier father. He'd seen atrocities and depredations I never wanted to hear about.

Wrapping my arms around his stiffened shoulders, I hugged him to me. "Is there anything I can do?" I felt helpless in the face of his despair. I knew he didn't blame me, but my being white would not help in the aftermath of this affair. I wondered if he felt he had to prove anything to his people, because of me. Leaning my head against his shoulder, I could feel the outrage pouring from him like sweat. He remained immobile, his face like marble.

"No, not for me. But I am afraid for you. If the soldiers come back, they may kill you. We must go from this place, and quickly."

My first thought was that I would never be among my people, the Kiowa, again. "Where will we go? Will we spend the rest of our lives running from the Army?" A thought struck me. "If I were not white, would you stay and fight?"

Finally, he wrapped his arms around me and drew me into his lap. "Perhaps, yes, I would fight. But you are more dear to me than life, so I know it is not because I fear the Army that we must go. No."

I could tell he was reasoning aloud. "You are precious to our people. Look what you have done, how you have helped, healed, in both our tribes. Because of you, they can see that some whites are good people. But I think, too, there will come a time when they will need your voice before the generals, to save them from rotting in the prairie like old buffalo bones."

I had not known my husband was a prophet. "Where will we go?"

Again, as we were before coming to the Comanche, we would be tribeless. I, who had wanted to teach the Kiowa the white man's words and letters, to help prepare them for life with the whites who were eating up their lands like hungry prairie dogs, had yet to teach any child but Magpie. That seemed a lifetime ago.

Stroking my shoulder, he stared into the fire. I touched his hair, amazed that he had come back to me whole. I dreaded the day when I would lose him, and

I saw, in a frightening vision, that I would. I did not know if I could live without him.

"First, I will see what Horseback has to say. Arrow Point is only war chief, and he must consult with the others." I knew that Horseback had gone with his family to the reservation to draw rations, leaving the war chief in charge. We were a tribe of about sixty lodges, and pulling up and moving on would take a major decision.

"If they choose to stay and fight?" I knew I had to ask the question.

"Then we must go. I will not see you killed by your people or mine."

"My people are Kicking Bird's, and yours." I was haughty in my response.

I could see I had hurt him. "You are right, my wife. Forgive me."

"I want to go home," wailed Hannah, breaking into our circle. "If the soldiers are this close, why can't you get me to them?" She was as demanding as a stupid child.

"I've explained!" I retorted sharply. "Do you want to die now?"

Johnny looked thoughtful. "Perhaps there is an answer, wife. What if you were to dress as a white woman and take her to the soldiers? You can follow their trail, it is as wide as a buffalo herd's. They would take care of you, and when life has returned to normal, I will come for you. I know it was Yellow-hair Custer who killed the Cheyenne, so I will know where to find you."

I didn't give his suggestion a second of thought.

"No. They would send me back to my father, and he would send me back East. I will not do this."

Watching us, her eyes large in her small-boned face, Hannah slid to my side and began pleading. "Please, do this. Please, please, please!"

I understood, but nothing she could say would ever tempt me to leave my husband, not even my compassion for her. "No, Hannah, it is done. I stay with my husband."

Something in my tone of voice must have convinced her to leave me alone after that. Gathering my herbs, I gestured for her to follow me and leave my husband to sleep in peace. There would be work enough for me today that I would sleep like the dead when I finally did.

I was grateful I was not Cheyenne, that awful day. And I was ashamed to be white.

Chapter 14

Harry Monroe perched on the wooden chair, his hands beating a silent tattoo on the arm as he listened to the Indian agent speak slowly and deliberately. His sun-worn face showed no expression other than fatigue.

"The man you've described doesn't sound like one of my Kiowa," mused Lawrie Tatum, running his hand through his thinning, gray hair. The kindness in the Quaker's face was etched with worry. "But I'll ask. Said his name was Johnny? I'm almost positive none of my reservation tribes use white names and speak our language as fluently as you say this one did."

Harry Monroe slumped in the wooden chair, his farmer's face impassive. "How long 'afore you can find out, sir? I'd like to be on my way, if there's no hope here."

The Indian commissioner stared out his window, the flat landscape far from the rolling hills and verdant cornfields of his Midwest home. When all this was over, he thought, I'll go home where it's green and growing. He didn't want to tell this worn, tired man the truth, that there was little chance of finding his wife alive.

"They should be in here, few days from now. Get their rations. I'd withhold them, if I could be sure your wife was taken by a Kiowa. But it would be unjust to do so, without more than you can tell me."

Monroe turned to stare at the vague point through the window that fascinated the Indian commissioner. "Think offering a reward would help?"

Tatum shook his head again. "I'm the only one who's gotten back captives without giving them guns. My methods work, I assure you, Mr. Monroe. I would employ them if I believed there was the slightest chance of success." His unspoken disparagement hung in the air between them.

"Mind if I ask around? Maybe someone's heard of this Indian. . . . If I can find him, could be I could talk him into helping me get into the Indian camps." Monroe's frayed shirtsleeves hung on his bony wrists.

"Don't be a fool, Mr. Monroe." Tatum was unusually sharp with the bereft man. "You'll end up dead. Times are uncertain; most of these Indians do not want to be on the reservation, we have not treated them fairly in the past or kept our promises, and you propose walking into their camps? I believe the angels go before us, Mr. Monroe, but even angels know where *not* to tread!"

Harry Monroe hefted the old Sharps to his lap. "Begging pardon, sir, but I'd walk into the devil's den, if I had to. You don't have any idea how it is, not knowing if she's alive, and what's happening to her.''

"I am not unsympathetic, sir. Do not misinterpret my caution for lack of compassion. But you must know the odds you face are not good.'' Tatum was beginning to tire of this man, so worn by the prairie and his own concerns that he could not see the total picture.

Monroe shifted and half rose, as though preparing to leave. Halfway up, he paused. "Can you tell me, Mr. Tatum, what the Army will be doing?''

Tatum wasn't sure how to interpret the question. "I am not privy to Army plans, Mr. Monroe. If you mean, will they search for your wife, as I have explained, I doubt it.''

"No sir, what I meant was, will they start killing the red devils who kill and steal from us honest folk?''

Tatum was slightly shocked. He knew his appointment had been part of Grant's peace plan with the Indians, to try another tack with them, one that involved education and compassion. But the fact the farmer was so blunt with a Quaker commissioner was not commonplace. Tatum decided he could only answer the man honestly.

"More will be done, Mr. Monroe, by the Army, I believe. I sense that General Sherman has lost patience, as have others who advocated a less bellicose response to the Indians.'' Tatum paused, wondering if he'd said too much. If *his* patience had been pushed to the limit, how much more so that of the political powers whose prestige and reelection were being threatened by a crowd of ragtag savages with outdated weapons? But his Christianity forced him to see the other side of the issue. The Indians had been sorely dealt with by his own people, and the plain truth was, had no reason to trust any of them.

He wondered if Harry Monroe had understood his response. Grunting an answer, Monroe hefted the Sharps into the crook of his arm and, turning his back to Tatum, hurried for the door.

"I'll start asking around the post, over at Sill. You hear anything, Mr. Tatum, anything at all about a white woman, you leave word for me there." Something grumbled in his throat. "Please."

"Of course." Tatum's words found only Monroe's back. He pitied the man, but he felt sorrier for himself. He was in an untenable position, a Quaker advocating violent and stringent methods to control those Indians who refused to surrender and starve to death on the reservations. He didn't know how much longer he could withstand the pressure within himself.

Chapter 15

I think they now call it the Battle of Soldier Springs. Whatever it was, its end result was the scattering of the tribes like leaves in a stiff October wind. Evans, I believe his name was, Colonel Evans, took off after the trail left by my people like a tick after a dog. Just as I thought, we'd packed up quickly, and left that place of the Red Moon, for that was what we'd all taken to calling the banks of the Washita, soaked for miles by the blood of the wounded horses running from the soldiers' guns.

Some ran for the Fort Cobb agency, where they prayed General Hazen would protect them. Others, like my husband's Noconee Comanche, chose the more traditional path and skedaddled for the open prairie. I understood why we ran, but it took me from Grandfather and Magpie once more. Hannah did nothing but weep. I had no sympathy, I was fresh out.

Johnny was the one who discovered we were being followed. The Comanche weren't ones to run like birds before the storm, so while we women packed our village as quickly as we could, the warriors rode out to try to deflect the soldiers from our camp. Johnny said the soldiers fought hard, but it was the howitzers that saved their hides. We hadn't seen such weapons used against us, and the blast of shell in our midst acted like a tonic. Everyone ran, throwing women and children two, three, up on any horse still on its feet.

Our allies, the Kiowa, from Woman Heart's village, splashed across the river to aid us. The firing from the soldiers' rifles was a rain of lead on my people. I hear that even today, you can pick up a handful of spent lead without even trying.

We divided and hid as best we could, but in saving our lives, we lost our village. They not only burned our lodges, they threw our supply of dried buffalo meat into the pond covered with lily pads. I hate waste, and white men seem to be masters of it.

Johnny wasn't ashamed, as I'd suspected he'd be. Very matter-of-factly, he explained how the soldiers, as night grew darker, had built fires and carried on with their camp as though the People weren't out there ready to shoot them full of holes. The war chiefs had reasoned that there must be more men than they'd guessed, for an enemy to behave so carelessly in the middle of a fight. They wisely gave pause and decided to move us out in the early starlight.

For whatever reason, Colonel Evans didn't follow us. I had taken Hannah and run as fast and as far as my lungs would allow me when the howitzers shelled our camp like stones from angry gods. I think, finally, she understood that we'd end up as dead as any Indian if we tried to pretend that being white gave us immunity from the soldiers. Shells don't discriminate where they hit.

I don't think I've ever been so cold, hungry, and angry in my entire life all at once. Those howitzers weren't aimed at the warriors, they were meant for women and children too. We hid wherever we could find rocks or trees, and that was where Johnny found us, Hannah and me. First Black Kettle's tribe, now my husband's, and in each instance, the Kiowa, my people, were drawn into the fray. Where can we go now? I wailed to my husband.

Johnny understood the Army even better than I, and I'd been raised around it too. "Go back to Grandfather. Kicking Bird will do whatever he must to keep peace with the soldiers, and you will be safe there."

I knew what he was saying. He would stay with the Noconee, and fight. "No," I answered softly. "I cannot do that."

"You must, for me." Taking my hands in his, he allowed me to see the despair in his eyes. "The end will come soon, for all of us who will not live on the reservation. I will not see you destroyed by my pride."

"Then weaken your pride, for my sake." I was ashamed of my plea, but I knew it was the only way he could stay by my side. A warrior could not worry about his womenfolk, and be effective.

Folding me in his arms, Johnny stroked my hair. "I would, if I could, Mythmaker. You know I would."

And so I was separated from my husband by more than a hunt for food. I cannot describe here, on this foolscap, how I wept when he could no longer see me, and how I hated my birth people, the whites, for driving this wedge between me and my spouse. I didn't even have a child to console me. For I knew in my soul that I would never see my husband alive again.

I was wrong. But the price we both had to pay was ferocious.

Chapter 16

Harry Monroe rode into Fort Cobb a tired and angry man. He'd spent Christmas in the saddle, dreaming of the wild turkey he and Hannah would have cooked, and the wooden bowl he'd been carving with birds for her gift. He hadn't even looked for it in the wreckage of their farm, the day he'd discovered her taken.

So far, the Army and Indian agents he'd implored to help him find his wife had been sympathetic, but nothing more. For a man who had the patience of a farmer, he was fast losing that part of his personality. Only the Indian with the fluent English who'd spared his life had given him any hope. He found it a sad commentary on things, all around. But someone had told him that General Sheridan himself was at Fort Cobb, and by jiggity, he'd get the general's ear if he had to twist it himself.

Rain and cold had made the ground well-nigh impossible to traverse easily. Plopping his feet wearily through the mud, Harry's horse showed the hard miles in his gaunt haunches. Harry dozed in the saddle, unable to keep his eyes open for long after his many sleepless, cold nights.

He accosted the first man he saw on foot. "Hey there, soldier, how do I find General Sheridan?"

The trooper stared at the ragged man hunched on a horse as tired as any veteran campaigner. "Well, mister, I guess you could aim thataway." He pointed to a log structure. "But no telling if you'll get a howdy-do from the gen'l. Busy day." The man pointed at a row of horses, most pulling a travois. "Indians here for their stuff."

Harry ignored the assessment of his chances with the Irish Sheridan. Pushing his horse for the last few yards, he wondered briefly at the shacks covered with tarpaulins. They were too small for men, not watertight enough for ammunition; he had the uneasy feeling he didn't want to know what they housed.

The feeling grew as he finally saw the circle of Indians, waiting like stones squatting on the ground. At first, he'd thought they were piles of rags, but when a hand reached out to cuff a wolflike dog barking at another, his gut turned to ice. He had them. Now, now, he'd find his Hannah.

His horse refused to gallop. Frustrated, Harry dropped to the ground and felt the mud soak into the worn edges of his boots. He had to find that general, and fast, before the Indians left, taking his Hannah with them.

"General! General Sheridan!" he bellowed at the top of his lungs. His horse, startled, hippity-hopped a few lumbering steps.

Harry began to race in the direction of the building the trooper had pointed out. Scrambling through the mud, he left his horse, reins dangling. Sliding across the last few feet, he crashed against the door, expecting it to explode open before him and reveal his Hannah, prim and neat in the general's presence. Rapping with his cold-numbed fingers, he shouted her name.

A trooper with a rifle over his shoulder cut the corner of the building. "Hey, what's the matter with you, farmer? Trying to break the prisoners outta there? Get back now, 'afore I have to shoot you."

Harry stared at the man as though he'd lost his mind. What prisoners was he talking about? Turning back to the door, he ran his hands along the edges, hoping to feel the vibrancy of Hannah radiating from its cracks.

"That's the stockade, mister, and you'd better do what I tell you! We got us some injuns in there, and them boys are in big trouble. You planning on a jailbreak?" The trooper wasn't laughing.

To his surprise, the door was locked with a huge blacksmithy's lock. Fingering the metal, Harry understood he'd made a mistake.

"But where's the general? Where's my wife?" Harry's mind was moving like water under ice.

"Don't know about your wife, but the general's over at the annuity. Indians come in today, get their treaty junk." The trooper paused and gave a small chuckle. "Lot of good it'll do them, is all I have to say."

Dazed, Harry settled into the mud again, trying to run where the trooper had aimed. He could see now what was happening, and only stare in amazement. Two Indians jerked back the tarps from the tops of the shacks and began piling bundles in the mud in front of two other men. As a bundle was hoisted, one of the Indians would call out something, and a man or woman would rise from his or her stone squat and advance. Catching the bundle tossed, each would return to his or her spot and begin rummaging through the pile. Harry watched as top hats and stockings, britches big enough for three men, and cheap black suits lay strewn in the mud.

When he was finally able to tear his sight from the bizarre spectacle before him, he found the small figure of General Sheridan off to one side, surrounded by officers. He'd seen the general's picture in *Harper's,* during the War, though he himself had fought in the West, with Grant before he took command of the Army of the Potomac.

"General Sheridan!" Running as fast as he could in the muck, Harry determined that this time, he would receive a satisfactory answer from someone in authority. "Need to speak with you, sir!"

The startled officers jerked into a protective circle around the general. Harry was undaunted.

"General, I need your help finding my wife!" Never a man for niceties, Harry elbowed a staff officer who attempted to strongarm him out of the way. "You got some of them," he nodded in the direction of the Indians receiving the clothing, "in that jail of yours, and I figure you're just the man to beat outta them where they got my wife, Hannah!"

Sheridan raised his dark eyebrows and gestured for

his officers to unhand Harry. Shoving at the tail of his jacket, Harry was unbowed and not about to stop talking until he got the answer he wanted to hear. "Been looking, since October when my wife was stolen, General, and no one's heard of a dead white woman so far, so I know she's alive, and if there's a way to get her back, I reckon you're the man for the job, sir." Harry may have been uneducated, but he knew a bit of flattery here and there wouldn't hurt his petition.

General Sheridan's blue uniform was impeccable. Even his boots hadn't seen a smidgen of mud. Carefully treading the boards laid for a walkway, he gestured for Harry to follow him. Some officers followed the two men, and others remained, staring at Harry's back and shaking their heads. The farmer wouldn't like what he would hear, and they felt sorry for the man.

General Sheridan gestured for Harry to take a seat in his makeshift office. Warmed by the immediate blast of heat from the portable stove, Harry felt himself becoming instantly drowsy.

"No, sir, I'd better stand," he replied, twisting his hat in his hands. "This shouldn't take too long."

"Young man, I think you should sit when you hear what I have to say." Again, Sheridan pointed at the Army issue chair, but Harry was having none of it.

"Well, it is my pleasure to inform you, Mr. . . . ?" Sheridan paused.

"Monroe. Harry Monroe. Wife's Hannah. Blond hair, twenty-five years of age, pretty woman."

"Yes, well, as I was saying, I am happy to tell you that the United States Army won a great victory not a month ago, on the banks of the Washita River. We have recently engaged the Comanche at Soldier's Spring. All these engagements have resulted in many Indian casualties, as well as captives. Those you see out there, Mr. Monroe''—Sheridan nodded at the annuity scene—''were on the reservation at the time these battles were fought, and so are considered peaceful. I do not want you to think we give supplies to hostiles.''

''No, sir, don't think nothing. In fact, I just want your help in finding Hannah.''

Sheridan pulled a cigar from a sterling humidor. Harry had never seen anything so fancy. Clipping the end of the cigar, Sheridan avoided Harry's eyes.

''There were, unfortunately, civilian casualties, Mr. Monroe. Our men discovered white women and children, clearly captives of these Cheyenne and Comanche, who had been killed before we could rescue them. Only one body matches your description of your wife, and I regret to say, we have not identified her. I can have you taken to her remains, if you would care to see them.''

This time Harry sat, and sat hard. Now he understood the officer's warning. ''Yes, sir, I suppose I do. If it's my Hannah . . . ,'' he began threateningly.

''Wait until you have seen the deceased, Mr. Monroe. Then we will talk again.'' Sheridan puffed on his cigar as he gestured for Harry to be escorted out of his presence.

''Poor fool,'' muttered Sheridan.

Harry shivered as he was ushered, by a quiet older lieutenant, into a small shack. A makeshift table centered in the small room filled his eyes. Gently the soldier peeled back the tarpaulin covering the body. Screwing his eyes shut, Harry prayed as fiercely as he'd ever done in his life that the woman wouldn't be Hannah.

"Mr. Monroe." Gently the lieutenant took Harry by the arm and led him closer.

Harry's first thought was that the black hole in the middle of her forehead marred her pretty face. Then he realized he was staring at a bullet wound, and he forced himself to look at the regular features and matted hair. Instantly, he released his held breath in a huge sigh. As he glanced away from her face, he saw another table, much smaller, covered with a similar tarp. They hadn't uncovered that one for him.

"No, not my wife. Don't know her." He wanted to run from the cold room and jump for joy.

"Then come with me, please, sir." The lieutenant held the door open for him.

Now, thought Harry, we'll get down to brass tacks. If I have to drag those Indians in the jail out myself and beat the tar out of them I'll get the answers I need. Returning to Sheridan's presence, Harry ignored the continuing annuity giveaway. He didn't give a hoot what the Indians got, as long as it wasn't his wife.

"Wasn't her, General." Harry couldn't wait to say the words. "Now, how is the Army going to help me find her? Figure you're top dog around here, I'll get what my wife deserves, which is your full attention."

Sheridan, while pitying the man his predicament, wasn't about to take orders from any civilian.

"This campaign takes my full attention, as you so

succinctly put it, Mr. Monroe. All I can tell you is, if my men find any white captive women in the course of their struggles against the hostiles, I will see that you are notified if any claim to be Mrs. Monroe. Good day, Mr. Monroe.''

Harry found himself unceremoniously shoved back into the cold, cursing all Irishmen who thought they were generals.

He was back where he'd started. He needed to find the Indian who said he'd leave word if he found Hannah. When he did, he'd stick to him like horsepaste glue.

Chapter 17

While I was glad to be back with Grandfather and Magpie, I was eaten up by worry for my husband. He'd placed himself irretrievably on a path that could lead him only into the arms of death. I knew where he was heading, and the Staked Plains were far from where I found myself with Kicking Bird's tribe, once again.

Hannah had finally tried to blend into the rhythms of camp life. I sent her on errands by herself very seldom, and she stayed often by my side. I knew she did so for her own self-preservation, as for affection for me, and did not resent it. I tried to teach her the language of the People, and I must credit her with trying. But her heart was not in it, and I understood.

The Kiowa split its camps that winter, and we found ourselves beside the Red River. This time, my joy at finding Grandfather and Magpie was dampened by the knowledge that Grandfather was growing old, and his influence was waning. Worse, Magpie was growing like a corn plant and would soon learn the ways of war. Unless I could intervene and stop his training, I would lose Magpie to the war trail, as I was losing my husband. I felt the anguish of women from all ages who sit and watch their menfolk leave for war, and are helpless to stop it.

Worse, I heard ugly talk about Kicking Bird. Women understood the politics of their menfolk better than men will ever give them credit. Kicking Bird was a strong leader, a man who had tried to lead us in a way that, frankly, kept us alive and out from under the soldiers' guns. But the women who whispered behind their hands were saying he had lost his courage, that he was as an old woman, content to stay by the fire and rest.

I couldn't believe it. Tending to a woman who'd badly burned her arm in an accident, I found myself being none too gentle as she slyly repeated the gossip.

"How can that be? He has fought often, and would not be chief if he hadn't earned his position." I tried logic in the face of gossip, and found, as is usually the case, it fell on ears sewn shut.

"But it is true! He would make us roll our bellies up for the white eyes to slice open and cook our entrails for a meal! He will take us into the arms of the soldiers, for sure!" She hardly noticed my rough ministrations.

I thought of Kicking Bird's pleas for peace with the whites, and knew he'd found war in his own camp, instead. I wondered what he would do, and realized there was only one answer for a Kiowa chief being accused of cowardice. Men, I thought then (and still do) are alike in their reaction to such a charge, unjustly made. They must prove themselves in some flashy way.

I felt I must do something, but I was at a loss as to my effectiveness. How to convince these good folk that further fighting would do nothing but kill off their families and hasten the end that was coming at them faster than a falling star? Magpie provided me with my answer—and my greatest fear.

Still a child, he would play with his friends for hours, tossing rocks and practicing with a bow and arrow. Hastening back to our tepee, I was eaten alive with worry for my husband, for my people. What I saw caused the bile to rise into my throat.

Magpie and some other youths had arrayed a straight line of sticks, frighteningly characteristic of a parade ground format for the troops. Shrieking with glee, they raced up to the line, touching their bows to a stick and knocking it over, then returning at a flat run to the starting line. I knew what they were doing— counting coups on the white eyes. I wanted to scold my foster son right there and then, but to do so would have shamed him irrevocably. Biting my tongue, I ducked into our tepee and fell weeping into Grand-father's arms.

He'd aged much since the treaty, but his arms were still strong and his voice carried the authority of his years. Between sobs, I spilled out my fear for all of us, my crushing sense of losing all that was good in our lives to a rolling stone of war that would not stop until all our blood lay in its path.

"Daughter, you have felt fear before. Is this different?"

I remembered the winter I almost died, how the old woman healer had finally felt pity and taken me in. My fear then was generated by despair. This feeling went beyond fear, into a hopelessness so deep I could not see the bottom to it.

"Yes, Grandfather. I sense we will all die before this is over. Kicking Bird is being taunted, and you know he will act to save his name. My husband makes war on the soldiers, and in a few years, Magpie will take up the lance and seek to make his name. I cannot see any end, but death. The soldiers are too many, and too strong, and their weapons, like the big guns which they shot into the village, will drive us under the earth."

Sighing, Grandfather soaked my despair up. "Then we must use what influence we have to make Kicking Bird see that peace is the only way we have to survive. I trust your visions, Granddaughter, and know you reveal them for love of the People. But I fear, after what has happened on the banks of the Washita at the Red Moon with the Cheyenne, that blood must pay its blood price before we will be heard clearly."

I accepted his assessment of the way it would go. I would tell my patients, and their families, what I saw as the truth, and hope that they would remember my words when the blood-lust finally died down, and despair bit at their throats with its harsh reality.

History has recorded my predictions. Kicking Bird mounted a raiding party into Texas that July when the sun was hot and the nights warm. Kicking Bird himself picked up a soldier from Fort Richardson on the point of his lance. The soldiers called a retreat, eventually. The warriors reported three soldiers killed, and a dozen hurt badly. I covered myself with ashes and waited for the soldiers to find our camp, and do to us what they'd done to the Cheyenne.

I had not heard from my husband in three moons' time. But the raiding did not end with Kicking Bird in Texas. Satank's eldest son had the stupidity to get killed by a settler in Texas, and the old man, with his evil eye and his twisted parentage, would take his revenge, I was sure. I heard that a white boy was ransomed at Fort Sill for a hundred dollars, and that the premium on whites was now high among the tribes. Along with my fear of the coming rage of the Army was a nagging suspicion that either Hannah or I would someday be dragged to the soldiers' fort to be exchanged for coin of the realm. Actually, I was less worried about myself than Hannah.

I had to do something about her, before she was killed by mistake by the soldiers, or by our people in a fit of anger. If Johnny were with me, I would have thrown her up behind him, and sent them off to Fort Sill, and to the Quaker agent I had heard refused to have guns protect him. If I did it, I might be seen as a traitor to my people.

I was almost ready to risk it, when the decision was wrenched from me by the United States Army and General William Tecumseh Sherman.

Chapter 18

Hannah didn't know what to make of this new camp. Mythmaker, as the white woman had told her to translate her Kiowa name into English, seemed happy and sad at the same time. But Mythmaker had lost that edgy air of distractedness. Hannah noticed she smiled more and was busy every spare second in visiting with other Indians, chattering over a campfire just like any housewife at home with visitors. Hannah forced herself to stop thinking of home; all it did was make her break into tears, and she'd finally figured out that a weepy face wasn't exactly endearing to these people.

Mythmaker had told her to stay close, so she did. But she watched. She listened. And she picked up a few words here and there, along with what Mythmaker was teaching her. She didn't want to be like these dirty, savage people, and she knew in her heart she was far superior to them, but she'd learned one thing. This white woman had survived this long among them, and she, Hannah, could emulate her, if that was what it took to stay alive.

She wanted to live more than anything else. Harry was out there, she could feel it in her bones. She hadn't pushed Mythmaker to get her to the soldiers after Mythmaker had told her about the whites killed in the Cheyenne village. But it wasn't because she was afraid of a white bullet. Hannah was sure that at the first sign of a white soldier, she'd find an Indian knife at her throat. So if she acted as much like the white woman as she could, she just might make it.

She wasn't sure if Harry would still want her, though, not if he knew what had happened to her after the Comanche took her. They'd never talked about things like that, even though there'd been long, quiet summer nights when they'd rocked in the front yard in companionable silence. She wondered now, with the constant threat of Indians, why they'd only discussed barricading the soddy, and practiced loading the shotgun. She guessed now that Harry hadn't wanted to think about what would happen if she should be taken alive. Maybe, she'd reasoned, he figured he'd be dead, and it wouldn't matter to him what happened to her.

Part of her was angry with him for taking her so far from any help, and for leaving her alone that day when they'd both smelled danger in the air. The other part of her was furious at the government, expecting good, honest folk to live in the middle of an Indian war with no help. When, and if, she ever got back to civilization, she'd find a way to get to Washington, D.C., and by jimminy, those politicians and especially the president, they'd have to listen to her. She'd scream from the front steps of the Capitol building, if she had to, what had happened to her. She had little shame left, after what the Comanche had done. And if the white woman, Mythmaker, could live with an Indian with what was clearly pride, then Hannah Monroe could hold her head up among decent people again.

She watched a lot. Mythmaker didn't make her work, but she found she was fascinated by the white woman's healing abilities. Once, she'd asked if Mythmaker had learned her skills at her mother's knee, and a cloud across the woman's face told her to ask about the past no more. But after a few minutes, Mythmaker explained that she'd learned what she knew from an old Kiowa woman who had died.

Hannah figured out that Mythmaker must not have been with the Kiowa too long. She spoke English as though she'd never forgotten the words. And the man she called her husband spoke English as well, much to her surprise. The one puzzlement was Mythmaker's obvious reluctance to go near the soldiers, or anything that would take her into contact with whites. What was she hiding?

Hannah wondered if the white woman was shamed by her savage husband. Had she left a decent white man somewhere, who wouldn't take her back? But when she'd seen how Mythmaker blossomed when the man she called husband was around, Hannah knew the answer.

So she kept her mouth shut, and watched, and waited, and prayed it wouldn't be so long that Harry wouldn't recognize her. She knew her hair had lost its luster, and she wasn't any too spotless, she who'd been most particular about cleanliness.

And when she got home, she'd hold her head up high and stare down any sanctimonious women who dared whisper behind their hands when she went to town. Because it took more courage to live than to die, and she knew it only too well.

She prayed Harry would understand, but if he didn't, it was his loss.

Chapter 19

Sherman ordered a Daughtery ambulance and a small escort, fifteen cavalrymen, for this foray along the Texas border. He'd told the president he'd give him an answer once and for all about the Indians and what to do, and he intended on moving fast and seeing much.

What surprised him was that there weren't more raids to steal the settlers' stock. "If the Comanches don't steal horses it is because they cannot be tempted," he wrote in a brief report.

General Marcy, riding with Sherman, wasn't as complacent about the lack of populace. "General, this place was packed double what you're seeing today, before the War. If our people keep getting killed, or scared off, at this rate, Texas will be nothing but sand and wind and Indians all over again."

They'd camped that night at Fort Belknap, along the old Butterfield stage trail, which General Marcy had helped lay out many years before the War. No one had used it as a stage line for years, finding it too expensive and dangerous. But Sherman seemed oblivious to any risks.

Sucking on his cigar, Sherman tapped ash into the fire before him. Ragged ruins and a few forlorn chimneys poked black fingers against the twilight sky. He'd seen a lot of sand, a few people, and some pitifully small hills these West Texans called ''mountains,'' but nothing to alarm him, not yet. He took Marcy's words with a huge grain of skepticism.

''Seems to me, best thing I can recommend now is that the few men stationed out here, in the middle of nowhere, be made more confident of their position. Jackrabbit jumps, they grab their guns.'' Sherman's disdain was clear as broth.

''Begging your pardon, sir, but they've got a right to be. Wasn't but a few months back the Kiowa killed Brit Johnson, and by golly, he's a man I'd have sworn would have dodged an arrow and died in bed of old age. No, General, when they start killing heroes like Johnson, and driving our men back to their posts with their tails between their legs, they've got the upper hand, not us.''

Marcy worried a bit about his forthrightness with the general, but they were both old soldiers. If they couldn't speak frankly, sitting before the fire with a mug of strong coffee in their hands, then the United States Army was in big trouble.

Sherman kicked a stray ember with his boot, sending a small spray of sparks into the sand. ''Heard much the same about the South, if you'd remember.

Better born fighters, natural shooters. Didn't work out that way, did it, General?''

Marcy knew Sherman was needling him gently. ''These Indians aren't Southerners, with a code of honor and all that blarney. They don't think like us, don't act like us, and they'll never be like us. Only thing we can do is get rid of them.''

''Heard that before too, and while I may agree, we've got to decide how and when, and how we keep the Quakers happy while we're doing it.'' Sherman tilted back his camp stool and stared at the brilliant stars splashing the early evening sky.

''Impossible task, if I may say so, General.'' Marcy threw his coffee dregs into the fire. ''I'll be turning in, sir. Good night.''

Running his hands over his face, Cump Sherman had to admit to himself that he was mighty tired of playing the political game when all he really knew how to do well was to soldier.

By 1:00 the following afternoon, the general's party crossed the head of Flint Creek and headed into the wide-open shooting gallery of land leading to Cox Mountain. With no cover for miles, and the mountain a good hiding spot for an enemy, the area had been soaked with blood many times. Sherman, no more wary than usual, was unaware a war party watched his progress. Only a shaman with a vision of large prey saved his freckled hide.

Greeted at Fort Richardson by Ranald Mackenzie's Fourth Cavalry, Sherman made camp in a tent and set up his desk to take complaints from civilians. Listening to their frenzied stories, he discounted them by 75 percent. He was still making promises to investigate charges that the Indians were getting arms and ammunition at Fort Sill. Grierson, he thought, was going to have a heck of a time getting the Texans to believe he wasn't abetting the enemy with U.S. ammunition.

After a supper with the taciturn Scot, Colonel Mackenzie, Sherman turned in for a soldier's sleep on his camp cot. Not too many hours later, he was awakened by a grim Mackenzie.

"General, you've got to hear this. Man in the hospital, says he escaped a Kiowa war party, killed seven teamsters and stole all their mules."

Sherman knew this was what he'd been waiting for. This was no stale story, embroidered by time and self-aggrandizement. At the hospital before dawn, he spoke with the wounded man, then sat down to write his orders.

Mackenzie's Fourth Cavalry was to investigate, pursue, and drive the hostiles to Fort Sill. Sherman would meet him there.

Chapter 20

I knew Satank as a vicious man with a scraggly mustache and rumors of evil spirits. It was known that his father's mother came from the Blackfoot tribe, and we all knew that they ate human flesh and were generally witchy people. I'd heard stories that he had killed, with his magic powers, one or two men who had opposed him in our tribe. But he stayed away from me and mine, so I had had no dealings with him.

But that May day in 1871, Satank ran the Kiowa down a warpath that led them to doom. Oh, I know how he and the others, Big Tree, Yellow Wolf, Satanta, crowed and preened themselves in their victory dance. I even saw the forty-one mules they captured, and heard how they tortured the man who shot Hautau. I wanted to hide in my tepee and stuff my ears with cottontails to keep out the horrid tale. The stupid fools had no idea what they'd done.

Grandfather kept to our home that day, but Magpie couldn't be restrained. I almost went hunting him, but

I knew his shame would be great if I hauled him home like a baby crawling too close to the fire. Rocking on my heels, I tried to grind my herbs, fresh ones newly sprouted this spring, and think healing thoughts. Hautau's wound was to the face, and I feared he would not live. He'd been shot when he laid hands on a wagon to claim its contents, and like a fool, stood there while a white man lifted the canvas and shot him point-blank. I wished for whiskey to clean the wound, but would have to make do.

Why did I try to help these men who were sure to destroy my tribe? I know it's hard for whites to understand, but perhaps you Army folk will see the wisdom in their ways. The tribe takes precedence, and all abide by tribal decisions, or leave. Just as when the general gives the order to move the post, everyone reports for duty ready to pack and haul, so too with a tribe. I was just one voice, and my dream of setting up a school and teaching the People the white man's ways so they could survive in a new world was just that—a dream. So I did as my tribe did, and I knew I would be there until the end, bandaging and cleaning wounds, and praying that the end would be swift, so that some would survive, particularly Magpie and Grandfather.

There was to be joy in my life again, even if just for a little while, however. I had hidden my loneliness for my husband, my nagging fear for his life, from Grandfather and Magpie, but it was ever with me. I sat by my fire one morning, not long after the mule train raid, praying as I stirred food for my family, when Hannah came running from the creek where I'd sent her for water. She'd been quiet these days, when I'd explained what I knew would happen as a consequence of the raid, and both of us were trying to figure out what to do with her. She finally understood the precariousness of her place and blended in as well as could be hoped for a white woman with long blond hair.

That day, she was suddenly no longer silent as a tree, moving quietly among the People. "He's here, he's here!" I heard her scream at me.

I had no idea what she meant and almost grabbed her from fear that someone meant her harm. Racing to her side, I brandished my stirring spoon, ready to beat off any attacker. Roughly she grabbed my shoulders and spun me around.

I could hardly believe it. Johnny was home, and it was all I could do not to drag him from his horse and smother him with my love. Instead, I ran to hang onto his leg, pressing the hand he politely gave me, smiling my welcome.

"Come, wife, we have much to discuss," was all the warning he gave me. But leaning over as he dismounted, he whispered softly in my ear, "I have missed you much."

I didn't want to talk, I wanted to be with my husband. Grandfather and Hannah, however, had other ideas, and as Johnny unpacked his horse, and Magpie materialized to take him to water and rub him down, I found all three of us seated around our fire. I knew word he had returned would spread fast, and the chiefs would come to discover what he'd heard of the Army.

But first, I wanted to hold him to me and rejoice he'd come back to me, alive.

"There has been much fighting, Grandfather," my husband began formally to the head male of our tepee. "The white soldiers are very angry, and everywhere I go, I hear that the chief soldier, Sherman, has come to make sure we go to the reservation, or die."

I caught my breath and held it. Hannah had learned enough Kiowa to understand "soldiers" and "reservation." Surely she recognized Sherman's name. I was afraid to take my eyes from my husband, however, for fear of seeing him vanish before me.

Johnny continued, "We must bring this fight to an end, and now. I have seen how the soldiers lose to us, but come back with more and more men, and that there is no way we can win. I had hoped to find a place on the Staked Plains for us, but even the Kwadhi will have to surrender, sooner than later. I did not die, and I have seen that there is a reason. I must help make a peace that will last."

I could feel the tears scarring my cheeks. This was what I'd prayed for, that my husband would give up his anger and help make peace. He'd suffered much at the hands of the whites, years of humiliation, and even my love hadn't been able to erase that. I'd known all along that he would have to come to the peace path by himself, I couldn't drag him. My husband, I knew, was a practical man, and when his pride was no longer in his way, and if he survived the raids, he would come to see the only answer, as I had done.

"You must speak with Kicking Bird," began Grandfather. He went on to tell Johnny about the raid against the wagon train, the dead whites and the stolen mules. Johnny nodded calmly and agreed.

"If Kicking Bird is truly on the peace path, then he must show it now, of all times. He must speak with Sherman. I know the white general has gone to Fort Sill." He and Grandfather rose to their feet to leave, and I saw that they were of one mind.

"What does it all mean? I didn't understand half of it!" exploded Hannah, after they'd left.

I tried to explain, and as I spoke, an idea grew in the back of my mind. I saw what we would do with her. Hannah would be a peace-offering. With Johnny's English to explain, the whites would surely see that Kicking Bird came in peace. Of course, they'd never understand that I'd kept her hidden for fear that the soldiers would kill her in a raid on our camp, but that was as it was. Johnny would have to keep me out of it.

"Hannah," I began, "you could help. Explain that Johnny, and whatever chiefs he can talk into going to the fort, want peace. Tell them." My words were forcefully spoken, since I wasn't so sure of her sentiments.

"You've done right by me. I'll do all I can," she answered, after a slight hesitation. Shoving her hair from her face, I saw, for the first time, a new woman. She no longer was afraid. This was good.

"You must be ready to go at once. Clean yourself." I handed her some grasses I used to wash. "My husband will see that you are safe."

I had no idea if he could get near the fort alone, but he'd manage somehow. For the first time, I felt hope assuaging my black mood. Happily, I found myself daydreaming about what it would be like when peace finally came, how we would start a family, and I would no longer have to fear being taken from the tribe.

Returning about an hour later, Grandfather interrupted my reveries. "It has been decided. Kicking Bird will go to the soldier fort. With the others. It is time to draw rations. I do not know how it will go, they are taking their rifles."

My golden mood was shattered. I knew what would have to be done now. I would have to go to the fort with Hannah. It was time I spoke for peace.

Chapter 21

By the time Mackenzie reached the bodies beside the broken wagons, they'd begun to swell in the Texas heat. Rain had fallen hard, and the burned wagons hunched like vultures, waiting for the final gorge. Slit grain sacks spilled their contents like vomit.

Surgeon Patzki dismounted, unhitching his notebook from his saddlebag. The report ordered by the colonel would be more a matter of counting bodies than identification. He used a stick to turn over one body, skull crushed, popped with holes like a pincushion. No, identification would be well-nigh impossible. Sighing, he licked his pencil and began to note the wounds and their position.

Troopers stood beside the other bodies. One by one, for all five teamsters, he carefully marked his diagrams with pictures of wounds, until he came to the man chained to a wagon tongue. Charred by fire, the cause of death was impossible, in such rude conditions, to approximate. Examining the remains more closely,

Surgeon Patzki noticed this one man had his tongue sliced off, and his soft body parts removed. He wondered what this man had done to cause such a horrible death. But, he noted with the grim determination of an Army surgeon, no death is pleasant for a soldier in battle.

They loaded the bodies in a wagon bed and buried it as quickly as they could. Scratching marks in a soft stone, the soldiers left only the number of bodies in the grave as any marker. Names would have to come later. MacKenzie wanted to ride, and hard.

But the trail was sodden, and a day late. Fuming, MacKenzie had to wait for the Wichita River to regain its original banks. Meanwhile, the Kiowa were building rough boats of willows and swimming their guns and plunder across. MacKenzie had no way of knowing how far behind he was.

Sherman was racing for Fort Sill as MacKenzie cooled his heels on the muddy banks of the Little Wichita. Met by an honor guard, he had little time for formalities.

"General," Sherman addressed Grierson, the commander of Fort Sill, by his brevet rank from the War, "we need to talk."

Grierson knew a command when he heard one. Escorting Sherman to his quarters, he allowed Alice to fuss about with lemonade and cookies for only a few minutes.

"This way, sir," Grierson said, holding the door for the general into his home office. Both old war-horses, they understood each other as soldiers.

"Ben, this wagon massacre has got to be solved

quickly, and the culprits punished. Mackenzie's out there now, and I need to know who in your command, or at the agency, will have the best idea which Indians need to be hung by their necks to pay for this.''

Grierson had heard the details and agreed with Sherman's assessment of the situation. ''Best bet is Lawrie Tatum. He'll have an idea, and if he doesn't, he'll do his best to find out who's guilty. He may be a Quaker, but he doesn't put up with this sort of thing.'' Grierson knew Tatum could be a hard man with the tribes, when the situation called for the iron fist.

''Fact is, I know he supports trying Indians who murder, just like white men, in civil courts. Problem is, he doesn't have the support of his central superintendent, not yet.''

''Good. Then may I suggest a ride to Mr. Tatum's office?'' In deference to Mrs. Grierson Sherman had chewed on an unlit cigar. Once outside the quarters, however, he lit up.

''Got a feeling, Ben, got one of those gut feelings this wagon killing's going to be the straw that broke the camel's back.''

Not until they were in the saddle, trotting to Lawrie Tatum's office at the Agency, did Sherman broach the subject of the commanding officer at Fort Sill providing weapons to the Indians.

''Bunch of nonsense, I know, Ben, but I've got to show something concrete to these civilians, prove to them the guns aren't coming from your ordnance.''

Grierson bristled. He knew the rumors, and they infuriated him. ''I'm sure our property records will suffice, General. I'll have them available to whomever you deem appropriate for a review.''

''Fine, Ben. Now, tell me about these Kiowa of yours.''

''They're not the Rebs, that much is for sure.'' Grierson began to describe the disparate politics of the tribes, and how even those who believed the road to peace lay in compliance with the whites were taunted into killing, just to redeem their honor.

Tatum was shocked when Grierson and Sherman recounted the wagon train killings. The square-jawed Quaker allowed as how he thought Satanta and some of the other war chiefs were off the reservation, and he'd find out more, when they came in for rations a few days hence.

Sherman waited, hoping for Mackenzie's arrival and a fuller report. By May 27, he was ready for another chat with Lawrie Tatum. This time, the Indian agent knew he'd have some answers, as it was Saturday, and the tribe would be arriving for rations. What he heard sent him scribbling with his steel-tipped pen, and a courier racing for General Grierson.

Col. Grierson,
Post Commander,

Satanta, in the presence of Satank, Eagle Heart, Big Tree, and Woman's Heart, has, in a defiant manner, informed me he led a party of about 100 Indians into Texas and killed 7 men and captured a train of mules. He further states that the chiefs, Satank, Eagle Heart, and Big Bow were associated with him in the raid. Please arrest all three of them.

Lawrie Tatum,
Ind. Agent

Sherman's response was quicker than a rattlesnake. Send them to the fort, he wrote, and I will deal with them. But Tatum wasn't done with detecting, and he heard that Lone Wolf too was a participant in the massacre. He decided to relay this information in person. He knew that Kicking Bird and Stumbling Bear were camped apart from the main body of Kiowa, as a result of a family feud. If there was to be a fight over arresting Satanta and Satank, he wanted Kicking Bird there to serve as a peacemaker. Before he rode for Sill, he quietly pulled aside his secretary and suggested that Kicking Bird should hear from a friend that trouble might be brewing.

He hoped he'd made the right choice. Trusting Kicking Bird to keep sanity in what he knew would be bedlam sounded like madness, even to him.

Chapter 22

We'd planned to get Hannah to the Indian agent near Fort Sill, but I should have known it wouldn't work. The day had begun badly, with a dead bird outside our tepee, and Johnny's best horse lame with a tender fetlock. I've never been one for portents of disaster, but that day should have made me mend my ways.

Wrapped in a blanket, even though the day was warm, Hannah and I set out, riding double on the old mare. I'd told her my plan, and that she must, at all costs, conceal my existence from those who would question her about her captivity. She'd agreed readily. I knew I would miss her, for having another white woman to speak with was a rarity I probably would never enjoy again. But the time had come when she must go. I didn't want a war with Kicking Bird to start because word got out to the Army that a white woman was a captive with us. I could feel the precariousness of our times, like a knife point balanced on the tip of my finger.

It was a beautiful spring day, I remember that. Despite the warming sun and the smells of a flowering prairie, I took no joy in what would normally have filled my soul with happiness. Everywhere I looked, I sensed danger and bluecoats, and my own return to the white man's world. But we had concocted this plan, Johnny and I, and I would do my part.

Johnny would go with the men to collect rations and ask to speak privately with the agent. We would come from where he hid us, when the time was right and he signaled for Hannah, and the crowd collecting bad food and shoddy gewgaws had trailed back to camp. Hannah would go quietly, privately, to the agent, and Johnny and I would go home.

I suppose I should have felt I was betraying my people. I had no idea what Hannah Monroe's sudden appearance would mean to the agent, or if he would call down the troops upon a people innocent of her capture in the first place. But I had kept her alive among the Comanche, and now my own people, and I was ready to be rid of the responsibility.

Hannah and I set out long before the camp was up and abuzz with the morning's chores. Magpie and Grandfather accepted my disappearance with barely a nod from their beds. They were accustomed to my leaving at odd hours to help the sick and injured. Hannah, being a slave, didn't warrant their notice. I should have gone with my husband to the agent, but I wasn't to know that, until later that day.

Hannah and I made a cold camp and chewed on jerky while we listened for the signal from Johnny to approach the Agency. I would send Hannah on her way alone and wait for Johnny to come back and get me. But as early morning grew warmer, and the day was closing in on noon, I began to worry. Swatting at the horseflies became a nuisance, and my shoulders ached with tension.

"I'm taking you in, myself," I announced suddenly. I could no longer sit on my haunches like an obedient dog. Tying my hair under one of Johnny's old scout scarves, I rubbed my face with dirt. Filthy, with my eyes down, I would be seen as just another dirty squaw at the Agency. I told myself all this and tried to believe it.

Hooking Hannah's foot in my locked palms, I tossed her upon the horse. Hiking up my skirt, I used her foot for a stirrup, and pulled up behind her. I daren't think about my plan too much, or I'd give it up. Driving my heels into the mare, I could only worry that Johnny had been seized and held prisoner when he told the agent that he had a white woman to return.

The Agency was simple, a spread-out affair of low buildings. Accustomed as I was to the regimental precision of Army posts, and then the sprawl of an Indian village, this unprepossessing array gave me a modicum of comfort. Best of all, I saw no troopers, not a yellowleg in sight. Hannah was jumping with excitement, but I pulled her tight before me.

"Stay put," I hissed. "You must hide me. I will ask of my husband, then we will see what is to be done with you."

She started to weep, and I could have strangled her. I tried to remain patient, however. Once, in her position, I would have killed anyone who stopped me from getting home.

We reined up before the largest building. I assumed from its size it must be the agent's office. Sliding Hannah down, I kept my hand on her arm like a bird biting a worm.

A white man came out to the porch. Startled, I must have jumped.

"Do I need an interpreter?" he began gently.

I glanced at his plain clothing and deduced he was a Quaker.

I mumbled in English. "Where are the men who came for food?"

My accent must have been too good. Startled, he stared at the two of us as though he'd lost a diamond in a floor crack. I ducked my head even lower and gave Hannah a shove.

"Tell him who you are!" I hissed softly.

Falling into the poor man's arms, Hannah commenced sobbing as though she'd been tortured. I could see we were going nowhere fast. "She's Hannah Monroe. I seek my husband, a Comanche who was here earlier today."

The Quaker didn't know what to make of Hannah and me, and all he could do was stand there slackjawed.

"Tell me where the men have gone!" I commanded this time. With each passing moment, my bones quivered with warning. Johnny would not have left me alone, so close to the white man, for any reason in the world other than he was forced to leave.

Finally, the white man holding the limp Hannah

managed a few words. "They've all gone to Fort Sill. Orders of General Sherman."

I knew then there was trouble. Ignoring his questions, I rammed my heels into the mare, forcing her into a slow canter. My heart raced ahead of my body, and my soul was already downcast. I knew of General Sherman. I knew what was happening, and if my husband survived, it would be only by the grace of God, not the scourge of Georgia.

"Wait, wait!" The Quaker called to me as I got out of there as fast as the mare could take me. "Tell me your name! I will protect you from . . ."

Jerking the scarf from my head, I tossed it behind me as I turned briefly and shouted, "Forget you ever saw me!"

Only later did I learn that Kicking Bird had been sent back to round up the other men in the tribe, after the first group, including Satanta and Satank, had arrived at Fort Sill. Kicking Bird, upon returning to camp, had told the women to be ready to ride out at a second's notice. But, honorable man that he was, he returned with the men he'd been sent to fetch. He could not leave his people, not even the troublemakers, to face a white general alone.

When I got there, it was as though there had been a sudden plague, wiping out the entire post. I will never forget that day, as beautiful as it was. The grass was green and fresh, boding well for fat horses this summer. Though I'd never before been to Fort Sill, I would have recognized it as an Army post from the many I'd lived in before, in my white life. Neat and precise, the shutters on its quarters sparkled with fresh

paint, the rocks with whitewash. Not a trooper was in
sight, not a child played in a dusty field, even the
horses were silent. I was never so frightened in my
life.

I wandered, until I heard the murmur of voices. A
small row of stone houses, the largest one with a second story and closed shutters, seemed to be the center
of activity. Some officers, and a few troopers with
fixed bayonets, milled in the front of the house, and I
could see, between their pacing, the earthen tones of
my people. Kicking Bird's voice, suddenly clear to
me, rose above all the others.

"Be quiet, say no more!" he commanded in Kiowa.

Dropping the mare's reins, I crept closer. No one
was looking behind; all eyes were on the ginger-haired
general tapping his foot impatiently next to an officer
with a long, wild beard and dark, piercing eyes. The
chiefs, arrayed on the porch, were seated tensely, and
I could tell some had fingers on the triggers of their
rifles held tightly in the crook of their arms. Frantically
I searched for Johnny and saw him at the edge of the
porch, leaning nonchalantly against a porch rail. But I
could tell he was worried.

Two Kiowa women, who'd come out of curiosity,
I suppose, wandered in the yard, not far from my hiding place.

"Psst," I hissed softly, afraid to call attention to
myself.

Startled, they grabbed each other and stared into the
shadow of the house where I hid. "Tell me, what is
happening?"

"Oh, we don't know, something about those mules

Satanta and Satank took. The soldier chief doesn't like it, but . . ." They shrugged, as though saying these weak whites couldn't do anything about it now, so why were they making such a fuss?

I could tell their eye had been caught by a door open at the back of the house. "Go and see, will you?" I gestured at the door. "If there is a way our men can escape through the house, if they need to make a run for it, we should know."

They didn't seem to share my concern, but I could tell none of our men would make it off that porch alive if the general didn't let them. If Johnny, who was near a front window, could go through it, to the back of the house, I'd bring the mare for him. I had no hope of getting close to his own horse. The house was a sturdy stone structure, and if Johnny could disappear quickly enough behind its walls, bullets would have a hard time finding him. None of this concerned the two women, frivolous creatures that they were.

But the open door was a mystery to be explored, and the two women sidled through. I relaxed for a second, trying to discern what was being said. I could hear, as his temper rose, Satanta giving a too-detailed description of how he and the others killed the wagoners and covered their bodies with burning corn. He even boasted of the forty-one mules and claimed he would keep them forever to remember his moment of glory.

"What about the man tied to the wagon tongue, and burned? Who did that?" The general with red hair asked. His question was quickly translated.

"No one." Satanta denied the torture. There was a vague murmuring behind from the officers.

I remember praying that Johnny would look around and see me skulking in the shadows. I planned to point to the back of the house and make the sign language for "horse," when a great shrieking arose from inside the house, and the air crackled with the shattering of glass.

The two Kiowa women I'd sent into the house came tumbling out, frightened and squawking as buffalo soldiers hauled them to the porch. The general, whom I guessed was Sherman from his thinning red hair, demanded that Satanta and the others be sent to Texas, for trial and a hanging.

Our people, as this scene and the words occurred simultaneously, roared to their feet, pulling their rifles to their shoulders. As Satanta jerked at his revolver, clearly aiming for General Sherman, Sherman shouted something, and the shutters of the house slammed back.

Black soldiers from behind the windows pointed their guns at every Indian in the yard, and on the porch, and the whole world froze. I don't think anyone breathed, until Satanta shouted for no one to shoot.

Kicking Bird jumped in front of Satanta, shouting that he was known to General Sherman, and that he had always tried to keep peace by making the young men stay on the reservation. He pleaded for Satanta and the others to be left alone, and that he personally would see that the mules were brought back to the post.

Dusting himself off, Sherman listened carefully to

the interpreter, who was botching the job and doing only a halfway translation. He replied that he had heard of Kicking Bird, and was appreciative of all he had done, but that today, he wanted the men responsible for the killing at the wagon train.

Sherman ended by stating clearly that "they will be hung, and the crime will be paid for."

I hadn't realized I was holding my breath until I began to feel woolly headed. But Kicking Bird wasn't about to give up, pleading that these were his people, and that he would have to die before he let Sherman take them.

The translator changed Kicking Bird's words, and made it seem that the great chief was afraid of dying with the guilty. I could have strangled him, for demeaning the chief's honor, but now, I can see that he saved his life.

"You, and Stumbling Bear, will not be killed—" Sherman began, when everyone whirled at the crash of horses running in the direction of the house.

Trembling, sure the soldiers were arriving with howitzers to shell any of the chiefs who tried to break out, I forgot all common sense and ran for my husband. If he was to die, I wanted to die with him. I don't think he saw me as the soldiers on horseback threw Big Tree off a saddle, onto the ground before the stone house. The soldiers' rifles never wavered as a bugle split the air.

"Johnny!" I screamed, trying to fight my way to him. But he didn't hear me as soldiers came running from every corner of the post, flying from behind every closed door, mounted men from inside stables.

I can still see the blue sky, almost the color of the Navajo stones, and the dark blue of the soldiers' uniforms silhouetted against it. I heard gunfire and turned to see who was being shot.

I could hear faint war cries and realized some of the People had come too late to help, and been caught near the unfinished guardhouse I'd crept past earlier. I darted around a soldier and crouched at the corner of the porch. I don't think anyone noticed one dirty little squaw; they were all focused on Satank.

The old chief sat calmly in the middle of the fury, announcing that he was an old man, and if any soldier should lay a hand on him, he would die right then. Kicking Bird continued talking to Sherman, pleading for his people, when Lone Wolf, who had been among those we heard fighting, decided honor was more important than escape. Galloping up, he handed out his weapons to the other chiefs and cocked his carbine. Kicking Bird ignored him, as though men like him did not exist in the world.

Stumbling Bear finally intervened. Praising Kicking Bird's wisdom, he declared that the others who had caused all the trouble were whipped and acting like women, but that he was going to be the first to die.

"I don't know what it will be like after death," he finished, "but I am going to find out." Letting his blanket fall, he stood and faced Sherman, who was still pacing the porch.

His bow and arrow were steady, and the old man showed more courage than the loquacious Satanta. No one translated his words fast enough, but his intent was clear. One of the women I'd sent into the house began to trill in praise, and he let fly with the arrow.

He might have hit his mark, I realized now, except for someone grabbing his arm, I don't know who, and can only guess it was Kicking Bird. Pulling his weapon, Lone Wolf aimed for Sherman, ready to finish Stumbling Bear's job, when the officer with the long black beard sent the general sprawling on the porch floor, and grappled with Lone Wolf.

I thought then he was a brave man, as brave as any Kiowa, and I saw later that my observation was true. On his feet again, Sherman ordered Satanta, Satank, and Big Tree held for trial, and the mules returned within ten days. I practically fainted in relief when the chiefs agreed to come up with the requisite number of mules.

I made my mistake when I tried to slip back to my mare. I hadn't been noticed because of the fracas on the porch, but as the three chiefs were led away in manacles, the soldiers must have relaxed enough to look around. I bobbed my head and made myself as small as I could, hoping that the twilight would create enough shadows to hide me.

"You there, you, woman!" The black-bearded soldier pointed over the porch railing at me. "You must go back to your tribe, now, do you hear?" He must have turned to look for the translator, when one of the buffalo soldiers grabbed me by the arm and pulled me upright.

My hair gave me away immediately. Their jaws dropped open, and one muttered, "Well, I'll be danged." I could have said much worse.

"Who are you, woman, do you know your name? Still speak English?" Black-beard shouted as though I were deaf. I hoped Johnny was already on his horse and riding away. I didn't dare look in his direction, for if our eyes met, he would kill the man who held me like a coat for sale at the trader's store.

This day had begun badly, with a dead bird and a lame horse. I should have known how it would end.

"Take your hands off my wife," snarled Johnny, not two inches from the trooper's face. I glanced up to see such fury in his eyes as I'd never seen before.

Time moved like clouds on a lazy summer's day. "Arrest that man," Black-beard ordered crisply. "Take the woman to the surgeon's for now."

"No!" I screamed, over and over again until my voice left me. They had to drag me, fighting every inch of the way, through the dirt. I couldn't see anything of Johnny through the wall of blue uniforms that separated us. I hated my father's people that day as I hope never to hate again; hated them with a hatred that spilled from my mouth with words I had no idea I knew; hated them as I'd not hated the Kiowa, even when I was dying in their camps, a lowly slave unworthy of feeding; hated them with a blinding hatred that knew I'd not see my husband again.

I cannot think of that day without feeling sick to my stomach, and wanting to cut my wrists. I must stop writing here. It is too painful to go on writing today.

Chapter 23

They locked the three chiefs in a jail, shackled their hands, and demanded that all the others who stuck arrows in the corn wagons be brought into the soldier fort. Hannah heard what had happened at the surgeon's, where she and Mythmaker were housed until something could be done with them. The orderly who whispered the goings-on shook his head as he related how the Indians couldn't believe what had happened to them, and how some had ridden out, threatening a big war, according to the interpreters.

General Sherman had decamped, apparently happy that he'd taken care of the "Indian trouble" in Texas. Hannah watched Mythmaker, tied to the Army cot with strips of sheets, turn her face into the mattress, and refuse food and water. While Hannah waited for her husband to be found, and to come and get her, she decided the least she could do was help the woman who'd saved her life from the Comanche.

Staring out the narrow window of the infirmary,

Hannah wondered what she could do to make a difference. Mythmaker wouldn't speak to anyone, not even her. Remembering how the white woman had protected and guided her, she forgot her resentment at having been taken from her home.

"I don't see how they can keep you here against your will," she finally said to broach the subject. Sitting cross-legged on the cot across from Mythmaker, she scratched her head. She'd gotten used to wearing the leather dress Mythmaker had given her, and the cotton undergarments and gown she'd been given by some Army wife bothered her. She squirmed uncomfortably. The corset cut under her arms.

"It's a free country, isn't it? I don't recall you doing anything they could arrest you for, and if they say it's because of me, well, I'll set them straight right off! Tell those fancy officers how you saved my hide." Hannah warmed to the subject. For once, she felt in control.

"I'll go do some talking, find that Quaker man who brought me here. He'll do something, he's bound to." Hannah knew a good man when she saw one.

Mythmaker's face, set as though cut from soapstone, lay brown and still against the rough sheets. Dressed in her Indian dress, she looked more Kiowa than white, even with her blond hair, Hannah thought to herself. Rising from the cot, Hannah smoothed back her own hair, neatly pinned for the first time in months. The pins bothered her, and she was tempted to shake it free. But a white lady didn't wear her hair loose like a savage, even if it was more comfortable, she reminded herself.

"I'll be back, soon as I can find the Quaker. Bring him here, to see you. Want me to?" Hannah was pleading for a response.

As though she lived in her own world, Mythmaker's face showed nothing. If that don't beat all, Hannah thought, here I am doing my best, and all she can do is stare at the walls. Well, she wasn't about to let anything discourage her, not even Mythmaker. Marching out of the infirmary, she headed for the nearest soldier.

"Ma'am?" The corporal tipped his hat politely, curiosity in his eyes. "Can I help you?"

"Need to find that Quaker man, the one on the reservation. Tell me his direction?" Squinting into the sun, Hannah held her hands over her eyes, watching his dark face carefully.

"Don't think you'll get far on foot, ma'am. You need to speak to the colonel."

Ahh, she thought as he marched on after another polite touch of his cap with his fingers, *I'm being treated like a sick child, am I?* Almost, tears tried to force their way into her eyes, but she reminded herself that she was made of sterner stuff than that. She'd survived the Comanche and the Kiowa, she wasn't about to be intimidated by any paltry colonel.

Marching into the largest building she could find, she paused inside the door. Smelling of hot wool and wood, ink and dust, she knew she had the right place. A young officer popped his head through a door, as though expecting someone else. Surprise, mixed with shock, crossed his face simultaneously.

"I'm here to see the colonel. Hannah Monroe, you can tell him." Planting her feet on the wooden floor firmly, Hannah wrapped her arms around her middle and set herself to stay awhile.

The lieutenant read her signals clearly. "He's right busy, Mrs. Monroe, but I'll see what I can do. Have a seat." Nodding at a straight-backed chair, he waited. Hannah held her ground in front of the door.

"Ok, hmm," was his only response.

She hadn't expected the colonel to come to her, but the lieutenant must have said something to pry him away from his desk. His long beard beating against the dark blue uniform, Colonel Grierson boomed as though she were deaf.

"What can I do for you, madam? I assure you, I've sent word to every town and Army installation within five hundred miles, to alert them if your husband is seen. There's nothing more I can do for now."

Swallowing hard, Hannah tried not to be intimidated. "Thank you for your help, Colonel, but that's not why I'm here. I want to see that Quaker fellow, the one I saw the other day at the reservation, who came out here when the chiefs were at that house. He needs to speak to my friend. He'll help her."

"Friend?" Grierson looked puzzled. "You mean the other white woman, the one who won't talk?"

"That's her. She won't talk, because you're soldiers, and you've taken her husband and put him in the jail. But she'll say some words to that Quaker man, is my bet, and maybe that'll save her life, 'cause if she keeps on like this, she'll just waste away and die, and I'd bet money on that, sir." Surprised at how effortlessly the words fell out of her once she opened her mouth, Hannah realized she'd said all she had to say, and shut up. She'd gotten used to keeping her mouth shut among the Kiowa, since she couldn't make their talk very well.

"Husband? Who's her husband?" The colonel turned to stare at the gaggle of officers gathering in the hallway.

"One of the men you locked up, an Indian with light eyes. Speaks American, he does, and he was aiming for his wife when you all grabbed him."

Grierson turned to face his men. "This true? We lock up the wrong man the other day?"

A graying captain spoke up. "No, sir."

Grierson turned again to Hannah, his face still impassive. "There, you have it, my good woman. Only the culprits sit in an Army jail, I can assure you. If this white woman thinks she is wed to one of the guilty parties, well, I sympathize, but there's nothing I can do about it. The law must run its course. She will be returned to her proper family, in due time."

Knowing her instincts in the first place had been correct, Hannah inched forward while the colonel made as if to leave. Stretching out her hand, she brushed his sleeve. "That's why I want the Quaker man."

Annoyed, Grierson turned to the gray-headed captain who'd spoken earlier. "Captain Woodward, see that this lady gets an audience with Mr. Tatum, will you?"

Now that she had what she came for, Hannah relinquished her position in front of the main door. Smiling at the captain, she waved her hands vaguely at her waist. "Any time would be good for me, Captain," she pleaded as he turned to follow the colonel.

Pausing briefly, he searched for someone lower in rank. "You there, Lieutenant Nolan, take Mrs. Monroe to the reservation, will you?"

The lieutenant looked annoyed, then resigned. "Yes, sir," he said and saluted. Woodward shrugged, after returning the salute, as if to say he'd make it up to the lieutenant later, but he had to be the one to take care of the unpleasant chore of shepherding Hannah Monroe to the reservation.

Lieutenant Nolan turned to find Hannah hovering at his elbow. "Perhaps tomorrow morning, Mrs. Monroe?"

Her face stubborn, Hannah proved why she'd survived when other women would have given up. "No, sir, now will do me just fine, thank you." Plucking at his sleeve, she guided him to the door. "Any kind of horse will do too. I can ride astride."

Sighing deeply, Lieutenant Nolan clapped his hat on his head and held the door for the woman in the badly fitting dress. Although he sympathized with her plight, he resented nursemaiding her around. The sooner he got this over with, the better, he resolved.

Ordering two horses, Lieutenant Nolan took Hannah at her word, that she could ride. In silence, they covered the rolling land to the commissioner's office, where he deposited her, without ceremony, on the front porch. Accustomed to Mythmaker's long silences, Hannah kept her peace. There was a time to speak up, and this wasn't it. She didn't want the Army to know what she'd concocted in the hours since she'd determined to help Mythmaker.

Tipping his hat slightly, he spoke. "I'll leave you here, madam. When you wish to return to the post, Mr. Tatum will see that you have an escort, I have no doubt."

Nodding her assent, Hannah waited for him to wheel about and leave her alone before she released a huge sigh of relief. Tugging at her bodice, she flung her sunbonnet from her hair and marched to the door. Rapping smartly, she didn't wait for an answer before shoving it open. Today was her day for acting as she'd never acted before.

She cleared her throat. Empty, the small outer office was furnished with simple wooden furniture. "Excuse me?" she tried.

"Yes?" The gray-haired man who poked his head out of another door startled her.

Stroking the strings of the bonnet, Hannah swallowed her fear. "Mr. Tatum? I'm Hannah Monroe, and I need your help."

Lawrie Tatum stared at the white woman, bronzed from the sun, her blond hair askew, gown ill-fitting. Something about her seemed familiar, and he searched for her face for a clue. "Ah, yes, Mrs. Monroe. You look well, may I say. The Army is treating you properly, I trust, and sending word for your husband?"

"Yes, yes," Hannah snapped. "I need your help, sir, with my friend, the white woman who brought me to you. Her name is Mythmaker, and the Army has taken her husband, and locked him up, and tied her to a bed with old sheets. She is a prisoner, as much as her husband, and it is *not* right, Mr. Tatum!'' Taking a deep breath, Hannah plowed on. ''I figure you can talk sense to the Army, being as you helped them get those Kiowa chiefs, and make them let her go, and her husband.''

There, she thought, *I've gone and done all I can do.* Waiting for his answer, she tapped her toe nervously on the bare floor.

Mr. Tatum seemed to be considering her words thoughtfully. Finally, he spoke. ''Come, let's visit my wife, Mrs. Monroe. I believe we can make you comfortable.'' Pulling on his hat, Mr. Tatum held the door open for her, gesturing for her to precede him.

Hannah had no idea if he would do as she'd asked, or not. Either way, she could hardly refuse his offer of hospitality. Anything would be better than sitting in the Army hospital, staring at Mythmaker's frozen face, wanting to repay her debt for her life but not knowing how.

''I'd be honored, Mr. Tatum.'' Slinging her sunbonnet over her hair, she followed him into the sun.

Mythmaker's fate was now in the Quaker's hands.

Chapter 24

I don't know how he did it, but the Quaker got me out of that blasted Army post. Using a pocketknife, he cut the bindings on my wrists and ankles, and picked me up himself. I wasn't fully aware, but I remembered later, with that part of my mind that noticed what happened around me while the rest of me lived in another time, another place, where my husband and I were free and the buffalo were plentiful. Carrying me to a buggy, he set me gently on the seat, then took the reins himself. The officer with the long beard handed him the whip, and they spoke some low words I couldn't hear.

Then I was free, the hot wind whipping in my face, my arms and legs aching from my imprisonment. I tried to speak to the man, but my voice wouldn't work. I knew it was just a matter of time, so I was patient. Closing my eyes, I reveled in the warmth of the sun, in my escape from the Army. Now, I knew I could figure out a way to set my husband free. But I needed to get back to my tribe, to Kicking Bird. He would send all the warriors he could gather, I was sure of it. I didn't want to see Kicking Bird as he'd been on that porch, just days ago, frustrated and shouting that he would rescue his people from the white soldiers, and that general not understanding because the interpreter was so bad, thinking that Kicking Bird was still their friend. Yes, I knew what I had to do, and I had to get out of that buggy as fast as I could, and run.

Stiffly I swung my legs over the side of the buggy and braced myself. The Quaker must have sensed my plan, because he pulled in that poor horse so fast his mouth must have bled.

"Where do you think you're going, young lady? You need food, and a hot bath, and then we'll talk!" His stern voice offered no quarter.

"Nothing to say," I croaked. "Got to get back to my people."

He wasn't dumb, I'll say that for him. "How're you going to get there? No, my dear, I'm taking you home. I'll do what I can to help, but you must allow me to provide assistance."

The gentleness of his words struck me to the quick. I knew he was right; I was weak, dirty, and horseless. The soldiers had taken the horse I'd ridden to Fort Sill, and I had no idea what had happened to Johnny's mount.

He continued. "Mrs. Monroe sought my aid, on your behalf. I must say, I think the Army has treated you badly, but they probably just don't know what to do with you. Would you consider telling me your name, your real name, that is?"

I thought about what he'd said for longer than he liked, I know, but it wasn't an answer I could easily give. If I told him my white name, he would probably send for my father or even Noble, if he could. As I worried the problem, an answer came to me unexpectedly. My father could help Johnny, if only he would. An Army officer himself, he was bound to have some pull with the powers who decided what to do with my husband.

Swallowing hard, I blurted it out. "Elizabeth McFarland. My father is in the Army, my brother, Noble, is an Army scout. Or was. I don't know where they are now, it's been almost three years, maybe four, since I heard about either of them." I felt strange, speaking English to this man who couldn't speak my other language, my real tongue, Kiowa. Had I said the right thing? Only events would tell.

"Thank you. I'll do as you wish about notifying your people of your whereabouts, of course, but you will need somewhere to go, other than back to the tribes. The Army will never allow you to return, you must know that." His tone indicated he understood my predicament.

I stared at the distance, watching ravens circle. Sparkling in the sunlight, their dark feathers reflected almost blue, like the uniforms worn by men like my father. This is another day for omens, I realized, but try as I might, I could not read the signs, or perhaps I didn't want to. I had been too long in the white man's square building, my soul being sucked dry by their cruelty.

I don't know how long I imposed upon Mr. Tatum

and his wife, but they never made me feel less then welcome. As glad as I was to see Hannah, and to hear her part of my release, I had more pressing concerns. I must record, however, that I was happy to see that Hannah had recovered her good sense, and was no longer the weepy woman who'd thrown herself, speechless and sobbing, into Mr. Tatum's arms.

For many days, it seemed, I sat in a chair on Mr. Tatum's front porch and struggled with what I would be able to do to help my husband. I had no idea what the Army would do to him, and the other chiefs. But whatever would happen, it would take place soon, that much I felt in my bones. Mr. Tatum was free with what information he had, never dreaming I would turn traitor to him. But I had determined I must do what was right for Johnny, at any cost.

The day came when Mr. Tatum told me the Indian prisoners were going to be sent to Jacksboro, the town seat nearest the wagon-train killings, for a trial. My heart sank when he said they would, all of them, be subjected to the white man's court and law. I knew what that meant, and so did Mr. Tatum. I don't believe he was totally sympathetic, when I pleaded that my husband was innocent of any wrongdoing in that affair, but he did agree to take me to Fort Sill to try to see Johnny once more, before he was carted off.

I planned my husband's escape, unknown to Hannah and Mr. Tatum. I would steal a horse from somewhere, for I was sure there would be curious onlookers vying for a chance to jeer the hated Indians as they left their jail in shackles. Although Mr. Tatum kept no weapons of the white man's sort, he had a collection of bows and arrows Johnny would have envied. I slipped one unstrung bow, and as many arrows as I could conceal, into the room the Tatums had given me for my own. I wrapped a gut string for the bow around my waist, under my dress.

I had no time for Hannah, although she sought out my company daily. I had to think, and think clearly, and her longing for her husband was so palpable, it distracted me. I could not afford sentiment; I needed to rationally and coolly figure out whom I would have to kill first to free my husband.

I knew, once I killed, I could never be a shaman, a true healer, again. But the price was worth my husband. I will never forget the evening, when we sat at dinner at the Tatum's square table in their square house, and after the blessing was given, Lawrie Tatum fixed me with his dark, piercing eyes. I knew it wouldn't be good news.

"They're to be taken tomorrow, your husband and the others. I believe I can get you a short interview with him, your husband, that is. I wrote to Colonel Grierson, and he's not unfeeling. You must be at the post by early morning, you can see him at 8:00 A.M."

I had been forcing myself to eat, to gather strength for what I must do, but now I set aside the fork and rested my hands in my lap. I was praying, as I'd never prayed before, for the men I must kill, and for forgiveness. That night, I asked Hannah for the loan of one of her calico dresses. She looked surprised, but didn't ask me why, now of all times, I wanted to look white. Perhaps she thought I didn't want any ridicule from the settlers gathered at the post for the big event, which I would have received wearing my own clothes.

That night, I borrowed a needle and thread, ostensibly to alter the calico to fit me. Instead, I lightly stitched the bow and arrows to the cotton petticoat, close to the hem. If I sat carefully in a buggy on the way to Sill, they would be undetectable. Sleepless all night long, I saw my husband's face before me as I willed him to understand what I had to do.

True to his word, Mr. Tatum had a buggy waiting for me before dawn. I was in such a hurry, I almost failed to say a proper farewell to Hannah. Little did she know, I never expected to see her in this world again.

"Take care, Hannah," I admonished, "and go on with your life, even if your husband never comes for you." I don't know what possessed me to be so morbid with her, perhaps it was the knowledge that, if I didn't succeed, my husband would never again ride home to me.

"He'll come," she whispered fiercely. "Soon as he knows."

"I hope so," I answered, my eyes on hers. "Just remember, some white men don't want their women, after they've been with a tribe awhile. You tell him about me, and how you were safe. May make a difference." Here I was, about to commit murder, if necessary, chattering with Hannah about marital matters.

But we were both women longing for men not with us. I felt our bond more strongly that moment than ever before. She must have sensed my sorrow, for suddenly, she hugged me fiercely to her thin chest.

One of the men working for Mr. Tatum had volunteered to drive me to Fort Sill. To this day, I don't think that kind man, Lawrie Tatum, could have stood the sight of the tribesmen in chains, and that is why he forbore to accompany me. I don't remember much of that day, the weather or the ride, only that its events were to shatter my life as I had known it.

I could hardly believe my eyes when we got to Fort Sill. The women had come, some from every tribe, and sat moaning on the ground, rocking to their sorrow. Word had spread, I still don't know how, that their men were to be taken to be hanged by the white man's law. Riding past them in the buggy, dressed as a white woman, I was invisible to the very people I had nursed and cared for so intimately. I was just as glad.

The man drove me straight to the jail, where the chiefs and the others were kept. Handing me down, he backed up the buggy after telling me he'd be at the stables when I was ready to go. He too couldn't meet my gaze. I didn't care. Rapping on the door with my bare knuckles, I grazed them on the rough wood. I ignored the blood that seeped down my fingers, holding my breath for the jailer to admit me.

Rifle at the ready, he slid back the looking window. "Who you be?" he grumped.

"Mr. Tatum said the commanding officer gave his permission for me to see one of the prisoners. Johnny Two Hats. Looks part white, has light colored eyes." I kept my nerves out of my voice, at great effort.

"Yeah, I got word. OK, stand back." As he slid back the bolts, I wondered if he'd try to search me.

However, he passed me into a small, dark room, without so much as a glance to see if I held a gun. If I'd been in my Kiowa dress, they'd have ripped it off me and searched every seam.

"I'll fetch him," the soldier said curtly.

Glancing about, I saw no furniture. I didn't want to hurt the soldier guarding my husband, but I needed to find some way to incapacitate him. I hadn't had time to steal the horse, but I would think of that after I had Johnny out of there.

The clank of leg irons turned me on my heels. I could not believe what I saw. My husband's hair, filthy and matted, hung dankly in his face as he shuffled into the room. But nothing could disguise the defiance in his eyes as he glanced around quickly. I could see he too was planning, ready to make use of any weapon he could find. I don't think that he recognized me at first.

"Husband?" I whispered in Kiowa. "My beloved, it is I." I couldn't help myself, I ran for his arms, until the soldier shoved his way between us. I could get no closer than a yard.

"Mythmaker? What are you doing here? They will keep you forever, you must flee!" Glaring at the soldier, his voice was still tender to me.

"No, my love, I will stay with you. I will find a way." Reaching across the distance with hands that could not touch, I knew I should be telling him about the weapons hidden under my skirt, not talking of love.

"What's that jabbering? No one said you could talk

with the prisoner, just see him. Now get back, lady!''
the trooper snapped.

"I'm only conveying my regrets at his condition!
Surely you can have no objection." I put on my best
finishing school voice, the tone I hadn't used in years.
I was gratified to see it still had the same effect.

Confused, he'd stepped back, leaving the space between Johnny and me unguarded. Quickly I rushed
into my husband's arms, whispering about the arrows
and bow sewn in the petticoats. Although the trooper
frowned, I pretended I whispered only words of love,
as Johnny bent his ears to my lips.

"No, wife, I will not risk you, not here with this
man with his gun. If you can find a way to get them
near the wagons they'll use to take us away, I will do
what I can. But we are heavily guarded, every instant,
even in the rooms where we are locked in."

Smiling, as though he'd told me of his undying pas-
sion, I answered sweetly, "I'll try. I have a knife in
this pocket in my apron." Leaning closer, I guided his
hand to my waist. Even though his wrists were bound,
he slipped the knife into his fingers and hid them.

The guard had had enough. Shoving his rifle between us, he realized his mistake as Johnny grabbed
the barrel and shoved it into the man's chest, sending
him sprawling. I froze as the guard shouted for help.

"Go!" Johnny demanded, and I watched helplessly
as soldiers ran from the other door, striking my husband from behind with their rifle butts. Johnny's head
jerked as he slumped to his knees.

I couldn't stand there and do nothing. Surely you
understand that I had to help my husband. Flailing out,

I was myself knocked to the ground, then thrown unceremoniously out the door into the dirt. Weeping, I
realized I hadn't helped my husband at all, I'd probably caused him more harm. Worse, never before in
my life had I consciously tried to hurt another human
being. That day, however, I would have killed.

I had to find the wagons they would use to carry
the chiefs away; I didn't have time to lie there weeping
into the dirt. Pulling myself up, I was surprised to feel
the arrows were still straight within the folds of cloth.
Running, I knew I had little time to find the wagons.
Dawn was long past as the sun rose in the sky for
what would be a bright day. But I saw nothing more
than the slipping away of the minutes that would take
my husband from me forever.

I was too late, I realized, as two wagons rattled up
to the jail. I could only stand in the crowd that quickly
gathered, Army officers, soldiers on horseback, and a
man I thought was a Caddo. I had been so naive, I
realized, believing I could rescue my husband single-
handedly. Tears blinding my eyes, I stood helplessly
in the crowd as the door to the jail opened slowly, and
an officer pulled Satank outside. Chained and hobbled,
the old chief blinked rapidly, as though he hadn't seen
sunlight in many days.

The colonel with the beard, Grierson, stood in the
forefront of the other officers. I thought at first Satank
was trying to plead his case as he lunged forward, but
the sun caught the edge of a knife. He'd managed to
find a weapon, I rejoiced, for now there would be a
fight for our tribe's chiefs! Inching forward, I pre-

pared, slipping my hands lower on my skirts. I could rip the petticoats off in a second.

But the others, Satanta and Big Tree, jerked Satank back, warning him to stay calm and make no trouble. I could hardly believe what I was hearing. Satank not fighting? Truly, the Kiowa were at the end of their time on this earth. I despaired as the other men climbed into the wagon without a protest.

But I was not proven wrong. Satank, refusing to cooperate, was thrown by his hands and feet into another wagon, shouting that he was Ko-eet-senko, one of the ten most brave men in the tribe, and there was no honor today for him. I knew what to expect next, even if the whites did not, and I sank to my knees to pray for his soul. No one noticed me; every eye followed the wagon as it pulled out, with Satank loudly singing the death song of the warrior society.

"Oh, sun, you remain forever, but we Ko-eet-senko must die."

The rest of the men were loaded into the other wagon, my husband dragged with his toes in the dirt. I saw his head roll, as he was tossed facefirst onto the wagon bed, and knew he was not conscious of what was happening around him. Part of me rejoiced that he would not remember this infamous day, but the other part wanted him awake and able to fight. How could I get his weapons to him, if he was not able to hold them?

I seethed with impatience. The colonels, Grierson and Mackenzie, walked aways off to talk, so I followed the caravan of soldiers and wagons down the road leading to Jacksboro. No one tried to stop me, as

I stayed just far enough back to see the wagons. Running in the dirt, I decided I would run with them across all of Texas, if necessary. Blood pounded in my ears, my white woman's boots pinching, I became vaguely aware that the women from the tribe had begun to trill their voices. I knew what that meant—they were urging a chief to fight for his honor.

Satank's voice, strong and proud, carried across the miles. I only hope his words flew with the wind, to every lodge in every tribe. He spoke in Comanche, which surprised me, until I realized he left his words as a legacy to be understood by anyone within earshot. Comanche was a trade language, and more widely used than Kiowa, I remembered. I listened carefully, so I could memorize his words for all time.

''Tell my people I died beside the road. My bones will be found there. Tell my people to gather them up and carry them away.''

Then he began his death chant again as the soldiers mocked him, whining in simpering voices. I could have killed them all for the dishonor they did this chief who was, despite all that I did not like in him, a brave warrior and a valorous man. The Caddo riding beside Satank's wagon dropped back, and I saw Satanta and Big Tree straighten against the wagon sides. They knew what was coming next.

Beside a tree in the road, Satank rose up and tried to wrestle a rifle from the guard sitting at the rear of the wagon. The bluecoat fell over the back, landing on his head, as Satank tried to ram a cartridge into the chamber. An officer shouted at his men to fire at the chief, and as they did, I saw him stagger like a grizzly hit by a Sharps, but he didn't go down. Again, he threw the rifle to his shoulder, trying to shoot it at the soldiers, when they fired at him again. I saw blood spurt like miniature roses on his shirt, his head, his hands, and covered my eyes.

I could hardly believe it when the soldiers threw Satank down from the wagon, propping him against the tree he'd used to make the beginning of his attack. As blood rushed from his mouth, one of the Tonkawa chiefs asked for the honor of taking his scalp, but the lieutenant on horseback refused. Such is the compassion of the Army, I thought, still kneeling in the dust. Thank heaven, my husband didn't see what had happened.

I knew then it was hopeless. What would the bow and arrows I'd hidden in my clothing serve? No good end, not today. All hope drained from me as I listened to the wagons and the soldiers' leathers creak into the distance.

I had lost my husband, and I knew it.

Chapter 25

" "The impudence of Satanta will satisfy you that the Kiowas need pretty much the lesson you gave Black Kettle and Little Raven. . . . " General Sherman laid aside his pen and read through his letter to Phil Sheridan once more, stopping at Little Raven's name. With Satanta and Big Tree in the guardhouse at Fort Richardson, and since a jury of Texans already had convicted them for murder, it seemed that the Kiowa were finally going to get a taste of the white man's justice.

But there was the confusing matter of the man who called himself a Comanche, but who clearly had white ancestors, arrested at Fort Sill with the other disorderly Kiowa. The other chiefs disclaimed his presence at the wagon train massacre, but the man refused to speak in his own defense. His court-appointed counsel received spit in his eye as recompense for his efforts to help the man, and now the Texans wanted to know what to do with him.

What Sherman wanted was to concentrate on pressing for the advantage with these wily warriors who raided and killed, then slipped away like Mosby's Raiders into the surrounding country. Between the Comanche and the Kiowa, the Army had more than a full plate, and Sherman wanted the job done and finished. How this part-Indian fit into the picture is what he wanted to know. Should he press for charges to be made against the man, or let him go? Why, he wondered, am I concerned with this one half-savage?

He had to contend with the Quakers. Holding up Kicking Bird as a prime example of what charity could produce upon a warlike character, they still insisted that kindness and good intentions would bring the Indians around to a more peaceful frame of mind. Every time Sherman thought about their agenda, he wanted to drink, and it wasn't coffee he craved. Worst part of it was, Grant was partaking at the same well as the Quakers, and determined to give them a chance. Sherman didn't believe, given the reports of the unindicted Indian's conduct while under guard, that the man was innocent of all wrongdoing, and it went against the grain to simply set him free.

Mr. Tatum had sent the general a letter, stating that this particular half-breed was married to a white woman, who wanted him back. Although Sherman couldn't imagine such an event occurring, he couldn't discount the Quaker's statement in his decision for a recommendation.

What he really wanted wasn't going to happen, at least not fast enough to satisfy him. Picking up his pen again, he wrote to Sheridan, "Satanta ought to have been hung and that would have ended the trouble, but his sentence has been commuted to life imprisonment. . . . ''

Sherman knew of the Huntsville prison. If Satanta survived, he'd emerge a broken man. He thought again of the half-breed still in the Army's custody, since the Texas grand jury hadn't seen fit to try him. Perhaps he could use his attacks on his military jailers as sufficient excuse to lock the man up for a while longer. The fact the man had a white wife should be neither here nor there, and as far as Sherman was concerned, was a good enough reason to keep him behind bars.

At any rate, the man wasn't a chief nor, evidently, important enough for any tribe to claim him as a venerated member worthy of their importunities. The pleas of a single white woman and the Quaker commissioner were hardly enough on which to base any clemency.

Now that he'd thought the matter through logically, Sherman was pleased with his result. One less red man on the loose to commit murder on innocent white settlers was the way he felt about it. He'd finish the letter to Sheridan, then draft a separate document recommending Sheridan have Mackenzie see that the half-breed was locked up indefinitely.

Sherman rocked back in his chair and checked the scenery outside his window. Summer was in full bloom, and he was sure it would be hot in any guardhouse the military had in West Texas. Let the whole lot of them, every blasted Indian, learn that the white man's justice was hotter than any desert. As far as he was concerned, the man had been at Fort Sill when the chiefs were arrested, and that was guilt enough. Let him rot.

Sherman lit his cigar and watched the smoke float freely to the red damask curtains. These Indians would learn, just as the South had learned during the War, that fighting Cump Sherman was an exercise in futility. Mercy may be asked, but it sure as heck wouldn't be given.

Chapter 26

They had to go somewhere, Hannah decided. Mr. Tatum had read them the curt reply he'd received from General Sherman, as they sat across from his desk. Mythmaker had stared at the balding Quaker as though he were her enemy, and, embarrassed, Hannah had jerked her to her feet and shoved her from the office. Tossing a hasty "thanks" over her shoulder to Mr. Tatum, Hannah knew they were in deep waters now.

No word from her husband, and Mythmaker refused to do anything but stare at the horizon, snaking under a blue summer sky in the shimmering heat. Clearly, the commander of Fort Sill wanted them gone, but there was no place to go. She didn't know why, but she felt responsible for taking care of Mythmaker.

Pacing the infirmary, where they still made their home, Hannah stared at the officers' wives chatting on a porch across the parade ground. While she and Mythmaker received pitying looks and some old clothes from the ladies, they got little more. Hannah was sick of it. At least the Comanche had ignored her, once she'd gone with Mythmaker. These holier-than-thou soldiers' wives had no idea what she and Mythmaker had gone through to survive, and she doubted if any of them would have lasted a week with the Comanche. Slowly Hannah grew proud of her survival, and disdainful of the women who looked down their pointed noses at her.

Today had been the worst. She'd gone to the sutler's to buy a few things they needed, and he'd refused any more credit. He told her maybe her husband wasn't coming, and even if he did, he might not pay up her bill. Madder than a rattlesnake stepped on with hobnail boots, Hannah was still storming to Mythmaker.

"Kansas. We should go to Kansas. My brother might still be there." Mythmaker's voice, low as a breeze on a hot day, startled Hannah.

"What? You have a brother still alive?" She didn't know why, but Hannah had always assumed all of Mythmaker's people were dead, except for her husband, of course.

"Yes. If he agreed, he could help talk to the Army for my husband."

This wasn't what Hannah wanted to hear. "You know the Army is done talking about him. Sentenced him to prison, sent him to Fort Leavenworth." Pausing, she realized what Mythmaker was up to. *Kansas, and her brother, my foot,* she thought.

"What makes you think Kansas will get me any closer to *my* husband?" Hannah asked. "If I stay put, he'll find me, eventually."

Springing to her feet from the edge of the cot,

Mythmaker seethed with unleashed anger. "If we stay here, they'll kill us with their contempt. No, we must go. If I go alone, I will find a way to Kansas."

Hannah knew she was right. Mythmaker may have lived with the Indians half her life, and Hannah wasn't sure how long she'd been with them, not for certain. But in the eyes of the white world, one week or one lifetime was the same. They were to be pitied and shunned. What they needed were their lives back. Hannah could have wept for her simple little ranch, her quiet days of work and more work. At least she'd known who she was, and what was expected of her. She felt lost in a world where she had no rightful place.

"How're we going to get there? We can't even buy a bar of soap from the sutler." Arms on her hips, Hannah wanted to be difficult. Truth was, if she lost Mythmaker, she'd be losing her only friend.

"I'll find a way. Get us some horses. You ready?"

With a start, Hannah realized Mythmaker was serious. "Now? You mean right this minute?"

"No time like the present, my father used to say." Sweeping to the infirmary door, Mythmaker turned and stared at Hannah. "Don't worry about me, I'll be back. May take a while, but I'll have what we need to get started."

Hannah watched her stride across the ground, as though she were a miniature tornado, the faded calico of her dress flapping behind her like its tail. She has that way about her, Hannah thought, she can carry the land, the tides, the sun and clouds with her when she makes up her mind. Part of her was pleased that the disconsolate, broken woman who wept for her imprisoned husband was gone, and the old Mythmaker was back.

"Where are you going?" Hannah shouted, not caring who heard.

"Home," was the only answer she got.

Chapter 27

I almost starved to death, and I would have killed to be wearing my leather dress and moccasins, but I found them, finally. My people had run from the Army after the episode on the front porch of the colonel's house, but I knew I could track them. I had no idea where Johnny's people had gone, but I guessed the Staked Plains. My family was on the banks of Long Tree Creek, an offshoot of the Red River, with Kicking Bird.

By the time I found them, I looked as bad as when I'd been captured, and probably acted just as crazy. Difference was, then I was playacting, and now I wasn't so sure it wasn't my real state of affairs.

The commanding officer of Fort Sill had refused my request to send me to Fort Richardson for my husband's trial, and Lawrie Tatum hadn't felt he could go against the colonel's wishes. Why I didn't steal a horse and thumb my nose at them both, is beyond me. I guess that living in white clothes, in a white man's square building, had addled my brains until they were like pudding. It took me a while to think clearly, but once I made up my mind, I was sure of my path. Hannah had cared for me to the best of her ability, while I was sitting around letting my mind live in the past, and I owed her for that. I figured I'd let her in on my plans and take her along, as repayment. She hadn't yet figured out her husband was dead, or had found another woman by now. I just decided I'd have her on my hands the rest of my life, so I may as well get on with it. So I took off to find the only people who would help me.

I couldn't believe I'd actually stumbled onto my village. Waving my hands above my head, I shouted my name in Kiowa to the village guards who'd seen me. The prairie grasses waved around me, sighing their welcome. Galloping to my side, they touched my shoulders with their fingertips, a gentle greeting that said more than words. Without much folderol, I was thrown up behind one of the guards. Smelling horse, woodsmoke in his hair, all the familiar scents of my people, I almost wept.

I did weep when I saw Grandfather. He seemed to have shrunk in the weeks I'd been gone, and I could barely stop my tears from drowning us both. As a crowd gathered around us, patting our shoulders, whispering hellos, I was so loath to leave my people I almost couldn't find the words to ask for the horses.

But I had to. Ask, that is. Finally, we were allowed to duck into Grandfather's tepee. Alone under its hide walls, a slight afternoon breeze blowing through the smoke hole, I gestured at my white garb and shrugged.

"They took my clothes, at Fort Sill. Gave me these. Do you think anyone can spare me a dress, a real one?" I knew that would make Grandfather laugh, and it did.

"My, you have always cared how you looked, Daughter, and I just realized it!" He was trying to jest with me, a good sign.

Taking his hand in mine, I tried to keep on smiling. "I wish I could stay home with you, Grandfather, but the white soldiers have sent my husband to their Army prison in Kansas. He does not even have the honor of being in the same jail with Satanta and Big Tree, in Texas. I must go there and see what can be done about helping him. I let the white Indian commissioner back there"—I tossed my head in the direction of Sill— "do what he thought was best to help him, but it failed. Now I am through letting the white men do what they wish with my husband."

"Ayee," sighed Grandfather. "You sound like a warrior woman, not the healer you are."

I bowed my head. "That may be true. But I must see what his condition is first, if I can get into their prison. If there is a way to steal him out, I will find it."

"No, that is not your way, Daughter," Grandfather whispered softly. "You must take the white man's road to free him, or you both will be killed. I have seen it, in my dreams, just as I saw your return to us. You were right, you know," he continued, "those winter nights when you said Magpie must learn white ways, to help our people."

Sucking in my breath, I could hardly believe what

I was hearing. Last time we'd been together, Grandfather had made it clear Magpie would learn the warrior ways. "What have you done?"

I knew before he opened his mouth. "A white man said he would send him to a school, a place where he would learn the white man's words and how to read and write them even better than he can now. He came from the reservation and used sign language to speak to us, and after speaking with Kicking Bird, we agreed this would be a good sign of our friendship with the whites. I do not remember the name of the school, but he took Magpie with him not long after they arrested the chiefs and your husband."

I could only imagine who the man could be. Another Quaker? One of Lawrie Tatum's missionaries? Chances were good, and while I wanted to weep again at not seeing my adopted child, I knew I had no choice but to accept Grandfather's decision. Perhaps, I reasoned through the grief threatening to overwhelm me, it was the best path for Magpie. At least he would live, and not die in some white prison or in front of a soldier's rifle.

"It is well," I reassured Grandfather, after I had worked through the loss in my mind. "We are too unsettled now, times are like gunpowder resting beside the fire."

I left the rest of my story for a later time. We had enough, the two of us, to think about. Grandfather told me about the raids led by the Cheyenne, and Comanche, and Lone Wolf's rise to prominence as a war chief, and how it was muttered that Kicking Bird had become as a woman on the prairie to the whites, and let them do with him as they wished. My time at Fort Sill had been spent alone, or with Hannah, and I'd heard none of this. Expected a war, yes, I had, if the chiefs weren't released. When Mr. Tatum told me of the chiefs' fate, I knew events would ultimately lead to a war such as whites and the tribes hadn't yet seen.

Much as I hated to leave Grandfather and all my friends again, I broached the subject the next day. I'd slept well, for the first time in over a month, on my own bed. Finally, I worked up my courage to ask for the loan of a couple of good horses, with no promise they'd ever be returned. Grandfather blinked rapidly, and I knew he'd seen this too in his dreams.

I hadn't dreamed in so long, I'd forgotten what it felt like to know the future, to understand the past. Without another word, he took me to the tribe's herd and ordered a small piebald and a gray mare cut out. I recognized the gray as his favorite.

"When will you leave?" he asked me gently as the ropes were tied around the horses' necks and he passed their ownership over to me.

"Today. I hate to go, but I have wasted too much time already." I was afraid to add that I knew my husband and his pride, and that I feared for his life in a military prison.

"I spent my time at the soldier fort sleeping and hoping the man who was friendly to me would be able to help him. Now, I have awakened, and I must do this myself."

I couldn't ask anyone in the tribe to accompany me. Hannah would have to do. Grandfather seemed to understand. I left before nightfall, leading the piebald, carrying a parfleche of dried berries and meat, not knowing if I'd ever see my people again.

I turned for one last wave from the crest of a small hill, the afternoon sun late in the deep blue sky. The golden browns of the lodges of my people melded into the prairie, and I would always remember how the cottonwoods sparkled beside the creek. The tableau was lovely, peaceful, and in harmony. While I knew the ferment of war lay beneath, I have always chosen to remember how lovely our lodges were that day, and to hope I might one day see them again in the same light.

Chapter 28

I have been two years now, in the house my brother built for me. While I hate to write of what happened when Hannah and I finally reached Kansas, I must conclude my tale.

I'd been right about Fort Larned. My brother and his red-headed wife were well known, and all I had to do was wait for him to come to me. Hannah was a different problem, however. No one knew of her husband, and although we had traveled many miles, asking for him, we too had no idea of his fate. I think she gradually began to believe he had been killed searching for her. However she resolved his fate in her own mind, she picked up her life from Fort Larned and decided to settle in Topeka. Noble gave her money, and I hear she has set up a dress shop there. I hope she prospers, but I have no desire to see her again. Her presence brings back too many painful memories of Fort Sill.

While I do not wish to remember Lawrie Tatum and

the reservation, I cherish my first sight of my brother after all these years. He ran to me, down the riverbank where I used to go to watch the wagons as they cut deeper and deeper ruts in the prairie on their way to take my people's land. I noticed a dark-haired man flying along as if he was running from the devil, when I suddenly realized who it was. Filled out, his hair longer, his face lined with smiles, Noble scooped me into his arms before I could say a word.

"I thought for sure you were dead," he shouted over and over, and I tried to hush him. I sensed people staring. Larned is still a busy place.

"Not yet," I replied, and from there on, we talked incessantly. I remember how pleased I was at his happiness with his Rebecca, my amazement that my brother was now a father several times. I felt then, that all would be right. How wrong I was.

His wife, when he brought me home after Hannah had gone on her way alone, was kindness itself. Not saying a word to me about my Indian garb, she offered me a child for my hip, and a wet rag. "Clean his bottom, will you? I've got supper burning."

I knew then I would be part of the family, no matter how many years I'd spent with the tribes, or who my husband was. After dinner that first night, I drew Noble outside his snug little home, so I could ask my favor. I needed him to secure Johnny's release. He and Johnny had been so close, growing up together as they scouted for the Army. Their search for me had caused the one rift in their friendship.

"I would go myself, Noble, but you know the Army won't listen to a woman. If you or Father went to Fort

Leavenworth, Johnny might have more of a chance. They have no reason to put him in prison, not a military one. Who's head of the Army now? Still Sherman? Maybe Father could go to Washington. . . . ''

''Elizabeth, he's dead. Father, that is.'' Noble's words hung in the air like wisps of smoke. ''A year ago.''

''No,'' I wailed. ''He was still a young man, so strong . . .'' I'd always remembered him as a bastion of strength, sometimes too much.

''I told him you were dead. He retired not long after that, and I don't think he wanted to live. I buried him next to Mother, back East.'' Noble toyed with a corn-husk doll one of the children had left in the grass, not meeting my eyes.

I refused to become swallowed up in more grief; my life was beginning to choke on it. ''Then you come with me. At least as far as Fort Leavenworth.''

''I can't leave Rebecca and the children alone. Not for as long as it would take me to see all the people it would take seeing.''

I knew he was right. He had a farm and it took work. He had a wife and children who needed him. I was the one with nothing and no one. I was expendable.

Rebecca was the one who convinced Noble to let me go, I'm sure of it. In between cooking and minding babies, she altered a dress for me, a heavy bombazine that made me almost respectable, if I could ever lose my prairie brown skin. Rubbing lemon on my hands, she tried to soften their look of hard work and hard living. She tried to warn me subtly not to advertise that I was married to Johnny. Let them think, she hinted, that I was some do-gooder trying to help the savage red man. Play their game, tell them what they want to hear, she advised. If it got Johnny freed, who cares what subterfuge it required?

I must congratulate Noble, he married one fine woman. I am proud to call her my sister. In the end, I accepted her advice, and once more laid aside my leather gown and laced up a corset. Noble wangled me a seat on an Army ambulance heading for eastern Kansas, and I was on my way.

Fort Leavenworth sits on the brow of a cliff overlooking the Missouri River. A goodly sized Army post, it has a thriving town as well. I was back in "civilization," whatever that is, and as nervous as a dog with mites. The solid brick buildings, the large barracks, and neat expanses of streets, not pathways, put me in mind of a separate world. This was not the West, this precise, well-painted permanent place. This was a replica of Jefferson Barracks, outside St. Louis. I had entered the mouth of the lion, and if I wasn't careful, I would be consumed.

I found the commanding officer's secretary, a young man who stared at me in amazement when I named my request, to be less than helpful. But I had survived my capture by the Kiowa, so I knew how to playact. And act I did, just as Rebecca had suggested. I represented, I lied, a women's Christian group investigating a complaint about the treatment of a poor, ignorant Indian held in their military "disciplinary barracks." I demanded to see the prisoner and hear from his own lips his complaints.

Despite my sun-worn looks, my sister-in-law's best dress and my finishing school manners, arch and elitist, must have carried the day. I was given an appointment for later that week with the commanding officer. After leaving the address of the boardinghouse in town where I was staying, I resigned myself to a few days more of agony. I never doubted I would see my husband again.

I don't know where I went wrong. Perhaps I should have said I was his wife, so I could have seen his grave. But the next day a message was brought by a young corporal, who left it in my palm with a slight tip of his hat.

"Dear Mrs. Chapeau," it read (I had given myself a false name, in case McFarland was still known, and I would be connected with the story of my capture), "the man you inquired after had gone on to his happy hunting grounds." I almost gagged on the sly tone to the words. "I regret that any interview with the prisoner Johnny Two Hats is therefore an impossibility. Sincerely yours, your obedient servant," blah, blah, blah. I couldn't see the name for the tears. Was my life to be a flood from my own eyes? I felt my heart break as though an earthquake rent it asunder, and from that moment on, I ceased to live except as a shell of a woman.

Chapter 29

Another year has passed. I have swept through these three years since coming to my brother's house in a fog of memories. Last week, Noble told me that he heard at Fort Larned that Kicking Bird has died. The story being told is that he drank a cup of coffee and was dead before noon, writhing in agony. I can imagine that, with Satanta and Big Tree released from their Texas prison a year ago, Kicking Bird was not only hated by those who wanted to keep on the war-path, but also feared. Strychnine is an easy solution to ideological divisions.

I have had no word of Grandfather or Magpie. I hope and pray each day for their prosperity. I have thought often of trying to rejoin my tribe, but I have lost my faith. Without it, I would be useless to them, just another mouth to feed as the buffalo become scarcer than meteors striking the earth.

My hair, which I chopped off in mourning for my husband, has grown back unevenly. I hardly notice as it whips across my face in the afternoon breeze. I suppose I should tie it back and maintain the proper image of the contrite, despoiled white woman, but this black gown and blasted corset are as far as I will go. Rebecca sewed up the wound made when I severed my finger, a proper act of grief for my dead husband. I never asked for his bones, for I could not bear to go back to that awful place again.

Despite my lack of place, of position, of worth in this world, I remember who I am, and it says enough about me. I am Mythmaker, of the Kiowa, the fiercest, proudest people of the plains. I have seen their demise, watched the blood of the horses stain the banks of the Washita, healed their wounds when I could. There is no one to heal mine.

I will not destroy this box filled with foolscap and my wild handwriting. Perhaps my brother's children will one day read it and understand why their aunt was so strange, why people whispered behind their hands as they stared at her.

Maybe they will understand my pride in being the wife of Johnny Two Hats. I do not know what the years hold for me, but as long as I live, he lives in my heart. It is the best I can do.

Postscript

I felt it appropriate to add a postscript to my aunt's narrative of her years with the Kiowa. My name, too, is Elizabeth McFarland, or it was until my marriage recently. Since I am her namesake, I feel entitled to end her tale of her life as Mythmaker.

I was young when it happened, not yet ten years old, but I will never forget the day. My aunt, drifting through her hours with us like some raven, always dressed in black, seldom smiled but always helped with our family. Sewing, cooking, binding up a broken arm here and there, telling us Indian stories of the creation, she was like some exotic furniture made of different woods and strangely carved. We became accustomed to her part in our lives.

She gave me the old wooden box, tied with twine, for safekeeping before she left. She warned me that my father, her brother Noble, might not want me to know her life's story, but she said I would soon be old enough to make that decision for myself. Being

177

still a child, I hid the box with my other meager treasures, and as I matured, I forgot about it. Then, as I was packing to move to my new husband's home, I found the box.

It took me back to that day, when she gave me the box. I find I am not as comfortable with putting these words on paper as my aunt was, so I struggle for the correct words to convey the shock we all received.

You see, her husband came back from the dead. Well, not literally, for he was not dead to begin with. None of us knew, when we were children, that she had taken an Indian as her spouse. One day I was out picking blackberries with her, and I do not believe it was so many years after she wrote the last words herself on these pages. I thought of her as old, but that may have been because she was so somber much of the time.

Anyway, my Aunt Elizabeth and I were doing battle with the blackberry thorns, and losing if you count the blood they'd drawn from us, when suddenly she reared back and dropped her bucket. Annoyed at her carelessness, I quickly dived down to scoop them up, and she turned from me in a swirl of dark skirts. I remembered I smelled not blackberry, but sage, in that moment. I had never seen my aunt move so quickly before. Glancing up, I saw her long hair first, flying behind her like a golden sheet, as she twirled to face behind us. Perplexed, I forgot about the spilled blackberries as she ran from me as if someone had stuck her bustle with a pitchfork. She scooted right fast, for a woman who'd always moved very deliberately, very carefully.

I remember, I couldn't imagine what had caught her attention so quickly it warranted her leaving me with the blackberry-picking chores. I was right miffed, I suppose I should confess. Watching my aunt fly up from the creek bank, straight up the golden summer hill, I saw at first only her dark figure silhouetted against the tan prairie grass. I can still remember the crickets rubbing their legs like some chorus, and the crackle of the grass as she tore through it without looking back at me.

Then I looked up, to the crest of the slope just above us, and realized someone was standing there, looking like a fence post for all he or she moved. I wondered, as I noticed the figure wore pants, if my father had called us and I just hadn't heard his voice. But the sun was in my eyes, and even shading them with my hands didn't make a difference. I couldn't distinguish who the person was my aunt flew toward, much less hear anyone calling.

Even at that tender age, however, I sensed that something monumental was happening. Because I was loath to leave behind my bucket of blackberries, I trudged up the hill behind my aunt, following the swath she'd cut through the grass before me. By the time I had sweated my way close enough, I could see she was enveloped in the arms of a man with long black hair. I must admit, I was shocked and stunned by the picture of my prim and quiet aunt in the arms of a *man*. Thinking she was being attacked, I did the best I could, and flung the bucket of berries at the man's knees.

I must have screamed I'd run for help, because she

suddenly disentangled herself and swooped to catch me by my apron strings. "Don't run!" she ordered, her voice throaty, so that I could barely hear her. "This is my husband, and he is back from the dead." Her voice was almost a prayer.

I became rooted to the prairie like a jackrabbit that doesn't know which way to run. My aunt with a husband? I'd no idea. Now that I was at an angle from the sun, I could see the man looked like the Indians at the fort, who hung around the outskirts and were usually drunk. His face was lined, and the shirt he wore hung as if it had once fit a man two sizes larger. But when he turned to me and spoke, I knew this was no man back from the dead, and certainly not a drunken Indian from the fort.

My aunt wouldn't let me go, or him. Holding my hand, her other arm around the strange man, she led us both back to her house, where she finally released me. Asking me to send my father over to her when he came back from the fields, she once again melted into the Indian's arms as though she were afraid he would disappear.

I know now that she'd tried to see him, to argue for his release from the military prison in Fort Leavenworth, and been told he was dead. Evidently, the officer who'd written the letter hadn't wanted to fool with some silly crusading woman, and figured if he wrote that Johnny Two Hats was dead, it would be the end of the matter. I don't believe, after reading her story, that my aunt ever considered the possibility that she'd been lied to. She herself was too honest to see dishonesty in others.

I don't know what was said between my father, his sister, and her husband that night, but later, we children could hear our parents in their bed, talking softly until almost dawn. I rose early from the bed I shared with my younger sisters and ran to my aunt's house. I'd had a feeling I would need to say good-bye.

She had packed some saddlebags, and wore a loose man's shirt, belted over a leather skirt with a fringed bottom. I stared at her feet as she answered the door, saddlebags in her hands, for she wore brightly beaded moccasins that I'd never seen before. Quickly she hugged me and, handing me the box tied with twine, gave me the words I have related above. I sat on her stoop, digging my bare toes in the dirt, as the two of them drifted into the fading night, hand in hand.

It turned out that my father had gone straight to my aunt's house when I'd told him about the Indian who had come to claim her, and I will always believe it was to beg her and her husband to stay. When he came looking for me that morning, he stared over my shoulder into the house he'd built for her with such care.

My aunt's black gown, her corset and petticoats, were splayed on her narrow bed neatly. Nothing was gone, not even a cookpot, not a quilt. Evidently, they'd packed only food in the saddlebags. I told my father what I had seen, and he picked me up, big as I was, and crushed me to him as though I'd been a baby again. He didn't let me go, all the way back to our home.

He left my aunt's house just as it was that day she and her husband went away. Sometimes, he'd go up the hill and sit outside under that lone tree and watch the horizon as though he expected to see her marching back. As I grew, he seemed to take special pains with me, and finally, I figured out he was afraid that I, his sister's namesake, might take after her and run to the wilderness like a tadpole to water. But I am not like her at all, and I have married, at the old age of eighteen, the son of a neighbor, a boy I have known all my life. We, too, will farm this land, and I will never see the Indian Territory or any wild tribes for that fact.

My life, you can see, is nothing like Aunt Elizabeth's. Or should I call her Mythmaker? I believe so, and that is how I shall think of her, after reading her story.